CO-PRESIDENT/EDITOR-IN-CHIEF:
VICTOR GORELICK
CO-PRESIDENT/DIRECTOR OF CIRCULATION:
FRED MAUSSER
VICE PRESIDENT/MANAGING EDITOR:
MICHAEL PELLERITO

COVER ART: BILL GALVAN & BOB SMITH
ART DIRECTOR: JOE PEPITONE
COVER COLORIST: ROSARIO "TITO" PEÑA
PRODUCTION: STEPHEN OSWALD,
CARLOS ANTUNES, PAUL KAMINSKI,
JOE MORCIGLIO AND
SUZANNAH ROWNTREE

SCRIPT: BATTON LASH
PENCILS: BILL GALVAN
INKS: BOB SMITH
LETTERS: JACK MORELLI
COLORS: GLENN WHITMORE

WWW.ARCHIECOMICS.COM

ARCHIE FRESHMAN YEAR BOOK 1, 2009 Printed in Canada. Published by Archie Comic Publications, Inc., 325 Fayette Avenue, Mamaroneck, New York 10543-2318. Archie characters created by John L. Goldwater; the likenesses of the Archie characters were created by Bob Montana. The individual characters' names and likenesses are the exclusive trademarks of Archie Comic Publications, Inc. All stories previously published and copyrighted by Archie Comic Publications, Inc. (or its predecessors) in magazine form in 2008.

ISBN-13: 978-1-879794-40-5 ISBN-10: 1-879794-40-3

TABLE OF CONTENTS

RIVERDALE HIGH

I DIDN'T KNOW WHAT TO EXPECT FROM MY FRESHMAN YEAR!

RIVERDALE HIGH

My elementary years were spent in an all-boys parochial school that was three blocks from my house, and tended to be very provincial. But after I graduated from 8th grade, my parents decided to send me to a public high school. It was like entering another universe. It was so different from what I was used to. To my fourteen-year old eyes, James Madison High School in Brooklyn, NY had the look of an institution of higher learning, with a diverse faculty and student body. Its library had the ambience of arts and culture. There was a huge WPA mural in the auditorium (what's the WPA? Look it up! Didn't expect a quiz here, did you?).

A cacophony of musical sounds wafted through the halls as music students tuned up and rehearsed.

The football team seemed larger than life. I saw juniors with facial hair (the students in my previous school were much too young to shave). I thought the seniors came off as elder statesmen, I was young and sheltered at that point. The classes didn't feel like "kid stuff," either. Even the subjects sounded so very academic. While my old grammar school taught English, Geography and History, my new school had English Literature, World Geography, American History. I even discovered how mean a game of dodgeball can get. Then there were girls. Did I mention I spent my early years in an all-boys school? I now had girls for classmates. Another universe, indeed!

I hadn't really thought about my long-ago (how long? Trust me, long-ago!) freshman days until fairly recently, thanks to artist Bill Galvan. Bill has been drawing various Archie comics for several years now. He manages to give the characters a fresh look that is uniquely his own while keeping with the traditional Archie style. Let me tell you: he loves the Archie characters and it shows in his work. Bill also thinks a lot about the Archie characters-- and he realized that in the 60-plus years perpetual high schooler Archie Andrews has been around, there has never been a story about Arch entering Riverdale High as a student for the first time. Like a lot of great ideas, it was brilliant in its simplicity.

Bill even had a title for it - Archie: Freshman Year. And he asked me if I was interested in writing it.

Bill was aware of my writing from my previous Archie work (Archie Meets The Punisher and the "House of Riverdale" story arc) as well as my own series, Supernatural Law. We had collaborated once before when Bill illustrated my script for his characters, The Scrapyard Detectives. I thought we worked well together and I was flattered that Bill approached me with the Freshman Year concept. It immediately got me thinking: What was Archie Andrews' first year in Riverdale High like? How did he react to the school? How did the school react to him? Did he have to deal with bullies? Is that the year the Betty and Veronica quandary started? What was his first run-in with Mr. Weatherbee like? Hmm. Lots of fun possibilities! I told Bill I was on board and got to work.

Starting high school is a pretty big deal. It can be exciting for some, stressful for others. I admit, I was nervous. But I eventually got over it as I settled into the school year. I thought back to some of the Archie-like antics that happened to me and my friends: helping a lovesick buddy and having it backfire; running afoul of a bully charging a "freshman toll;" drawing comics during detention. And there was even a pizza place near the school where the juniors and seniors hung out. The place was always packed and it was intimidating for me and my "frosh" classmates to go in for a slice, let alone grab a booth! I thought I could incorporate some of those experiences into the Freshman Year story.

I wrote an outline for a story in four chapters. Bill worked up some sketches and did a fabulous job depicting how Arch and the gang would look in their very early teens. We pitched Freshman Year to Archie Editor-in-Chief Victor Gorelick during a very hectic San Diego Comic-Con International. Victor liked it and suggested we do a prologue to the series called "The Summer Before," featuring Arch, Jughead, Betty, Veronica and Reggie anticipating the first day of high school and the changes it would bring. The result was a five-issue series-within-a-series in the flagship Archie title.

This book collects the complete series. I hope you enjoy it. I certainly enjoyed working on the series and like to think I learned a lot from it. I guess you can say Freshman Year has been a real education for me! -BATTON LASH

WELL, THIS IS UNUSUAL, MARY...
WHAT'S THAT, FRED?
HERE IT IS, LATE AUGUST--
--YOU'D THINK OUR BOY WOULD BE MOPING ABOUT...
OH, FRED! YOU'RE FORGETTING THAT IT'S GOING TO BE DIFFERENT THIS YEAR FOR ARCHIE AND HIS FRIENDS...
THERE IT IS...
JUST WAITING FOR US...
WHAT'S IT GONNA BE LIKE?
IT WON'T BE LONG NOW--!
1

LET'S GO BACK, NOT TOO LONG AGO, TO WHEN ARCHIE AND HIS FRIENDS WERE ABOUT TO ATTEND RIVERDALE HIGH FOR THE FIRST TIME! ARCH AND THE GANG WILL ALWAYS REMEMBER...
The SUMMER BEFORE
FRESHMAN YEAR
PART 1 OF 5
WRITER: BATTON LASH
PENCILS: BILL GALVAN
INKS: BOB SMITH
LETTERS: JACK MORELLI
COLORS: GLENN WHITMORE
MANAGING EDITOR: MIKE PELLERITO
EDITOR/EDITOR-IN-CHIEF: VICTOR GORELICK
RIVERDALE HIGH SCHOOL
JUGHEAD JONES
BETTY COOPER
ARCHIE ANDREWS
VERONICA LODGE
REGGIE MANTLE
2

ONLY A WEEK AND A HALF TO GO UNTIL OUR FIRST DAY!
IMAGINE... HIGH SCHOOL!
WHAT'S THE BIGGIE? SCHOOL'S SCHOOL! IT'LL BE THE SAME OLD, SAME OLD... EXCEPT NEW!
YOU KNOW YOU CAN CHOOSE CLASSES TO HELP DETERMINE YOUR CAREER PATH...
COOL! MAYBE I'LL LOOK INTO BEING A SUPER-HERO!
YOU THINK THEY HAVE CLASSES FOR THAT!?
WHY NOT? IT'S A NOBLE PROFESSION! BUT ON SECOND THOUGHT--
HELP! MY CAT'S UP A TREE!
HELP! THE BANK'S BEEN ROBBED!!
HELP! THAT SUPER-FINK EVILHEART IS BACK IN TOWN!
--I BET THE HOURS ARE TOO LONG IN THE SUPER-HEROING BIZ! SCRATCH THAT--
3

--MAYBE I'LL BE AN INTERNATIONAL SPY!
TAKE THAT, DR. NOSE!
Hmm! BUT IF I'M A SECRET AGENT, I WON'T BE ABLE TO TELL ANYONE WHAT I DO FOR A LIVING!
I SPY... A GUY WHO'S NUTS!
I KNOW! I'LL BE A JOURNALIST! YEAH, I'LL LOOK FOR A CAREER IN THE MEDIA!
THAT WAY, MY NAME WILL ALWAYS BE PART OF THE NEWS!
I PROMISE TO GIVE YOU AN EXCLUSIVE, ARCHIEKINS, AND LET YOU INTERVIEW ME--
THIS JUST IN!
BREAKING NEWS!
PLEASE STAND BY!
SPECIAL REPORT by ARCHIE ANDREWS
KRIV NEWS
KRIV

--WHEN I BECOME A FAMOUS WORLD-TRAVELING BUSINESS-WOMAN, GOING AROUND THE GLOBE IN THE INTERESTS OF THE LODGE HOLDINGS!
Paris
Madrid
Russia
IT'LL BE A GREAT EXCUSE TO HAVE A JOB WHERE I GET INVITED TO LOTS OF INTERNATIONAL PARTIES!
HA! YOU GUYS MAY SETTLE FOR WORKING FOR SOMEONE, BUT NOT ME!
"I'M GONNA BE A CAPTAIN OF INDUSTRY, WHERE I GIVE THE ORDERS AND HAVE A LOT OF YES-MEN!"
TERRIFIC, R.M.!
WONDER-FUL IDEA, SIR!
YOU'RE THE MAN!
BRILLIANT!

YOU'RE GONNA BE CAPTAIN OF WHAT INDUSTRY, NOW?
Tch! YOU'RE BOTHERING A CEO WITH DETAILS, ANDREWS!
HAVE YOU GIVEN ANY THOUGHT TO WHAT CAREER YOU MIGHT PURSUE, BETTY?
WELL, I... AH...
THERE ARE SO MANY CAREERS TO CHOOSE FROM... I JUST DON'T KNOW! I'M GLAD WE HAVE FOUR YEARS TO FIGURE OUT WHAT WE WANT TO DO FOR A LIVING!
FOUR YEARS! GEEZ! THAT'S AN ETERNITY!
5

THEN AGAIN, THAT GIVES ME TIME TO LOOK INTO BEING A ROCK STAR!
I CAN SEE MY OWN BAND... THE ANDREWS!
THE NAME NEEDS WORK, BUDDY!
UGH! ARCHIE ANDREWS IS SO OBNOXIOUS!
HEY, JUG--YOU HAVEN'T SAID A WORD! WHAT'RE YOU LOOKING FORWARD TO?
OH... THE USUAL, I GUESS...

THE USUAL?! WE'RE STARTING A WHOLE NEW--
YEAH, WELL...
LOOK AT THE TIME... GOTTA GET HOME...

CATCH YOU GUYS LATER!

WHAT WAS THAT ALL ABOUT?
I GUESS HE REALLY HATES SCHOOL!
JUG ALWAYS SAID HE WAS ALLERGIC TO WORK!
YEAH--BUT I NOTICED HE'S BEEN ACTING LIKE THIS FOR DAYS!
SO? THE CLOSER WE GET TO THE FIRST DAY OF SCHOOL, THE MORE HE'S DREADING IT!
NO... IT'S MORE THAN THAT. I THINK--
YOU THINK? THAT'S A NEW ONE! WHILE YOU'RE GATHERING YOUR THOUGHTS--
6

I'M GONNA BE SHOPPING FOR A NEW WARDROBE! GOT TO LOOK MY BEST FOR THE CHICKS IN SENIOR CLASS!
REGGIE MANTLE! YOU ARE SOOOO CON-CEITED AND--
SHOPPING?!
I STILL HAVE SHOPPING TO DO BEFORE SCHOOL STARTS! C'MON, BETTY, HELP ME FIGURE OUT WHAT I NEED!
RONNIE'S GONNA BE SHOPPING RIGHT UP UNTIL THE FIRST BELL RINGS!
I'M SURE JUGHEAD IS ALL RIGHT... AND LIKE RONNIE, I NEED TO DO SOME SCHOOL SHOPPING, TOO!
AND SO...
...I'M GLAD YOU LIKE YOUR NEW BACKPACK, ARCHIE. AND THOSE SHIRTS WE JUST GOT MAKE YOU LOOK SO HAND-SOME! NOW LET'S GET YOU SOME NEW SLACKS!
SCHOOL SALE
BACK TO SCHOOL
SALE
BUT MOM -- I'VE ALREADY GOT SOME JEANS!
BACK 2 SCHOOL
SALE
SALE
SALE
SALE
RIVERDALE
DON'T I KNOW IT! BUT THERE WILL BE OCCASIONS WHEN YOU MIGHT WANT TO DRESS UP, YOUNG MAN...
I GUESS SO...
LISTEN HERE, YOUNG MAN...
YOU NEED A SUIT FOR SCHOOL! NOT BLING!
BUT MA!
ISN'T THAT YOUR FRIEND REGGIE?
AND IF WE MOVE QUICK, HE WON'T SEE US!

SOON...
...NOW THAT WE'VE GOT SNEAKERS, LET'S GO TO THE STATIONERY STORE -- THEY'RE HAVING A SALE ON NOTEBOOK PAPER!
YEAH, CAN'T HAVE ENOUGH NOTEBOOK PAPER! WHEW--! SCHOOL HASN'T EVEN STARTED YET AND I'M ALREADY EXHAUSTED!
SORRY! THE STORE'S CLOSED FOR NOW!
BUT I SEE SOMEONE SHOPPING IN THERE!
YES, THE STORE IS CLOSED FOR THAT CUSTOMER!
WHAT DO YOU THINK, BETTS? SHOULD I GO WITH SCHOLARLY SABLE OR THE LEARNED LAVENDER?
VERONICA, DEAR, THE PROPRIETOR WAS NICE ENOUGH TO GIVE YOU TWO HOURS TO SHOP IN PRIVACY, BUT YOUR TIME'S ALMOST UP! YOU SIMPLY MUST DECIDE!
I DIDN'T REALIZE HOW LATE IT WAS GETTING! BETTY, YOU HAVEN'T GOTTEN ANYTHING!
GEE, EVERY-THING IS SO EXPENSIVE HERE!
OH, DON'T WORRY! I'LL CHARGE IT! MOTHER SAID IT'S OKAY TO TREAT MY BEST FRIEND!
THANKS JUST THE SAME, RONNIE... BUT IT'S GETTING LATE--!
I HAVE TO MEET UP WITH MY MOM! SEE YOU LATER! 'BYE, MRS. LODGE!
SO LONG, BETTY!
RONNIE, DEAR, WHAT ABOUT THIS TOP? IT'S THE ONLY ONE LEFT IN VALEDICTORIAN VIOLET!
8

I KNOW RONNIE MEANT WELL BY OFFERING TO BUY ME CLOTHES... BUT I DON'T WANT TO BE HER CHARITY CASE!

IT IS FUN TO GO TO THE MALL WITH RONNIE... SHE'S SO INTO SHOPPING! IT'S ONE OF THE FEW TIMES SHE DOESN'T TALK ABOUT ARCHIE!
UGH! ARCHIE! TO THINK I USED TO LIKE THAT JERK!

Oh, I WAS SO NAÏVE BACK THEN... I THOUGHT HE WAS SO CUTE! I LIKED HIM SO MUCH!
SALE

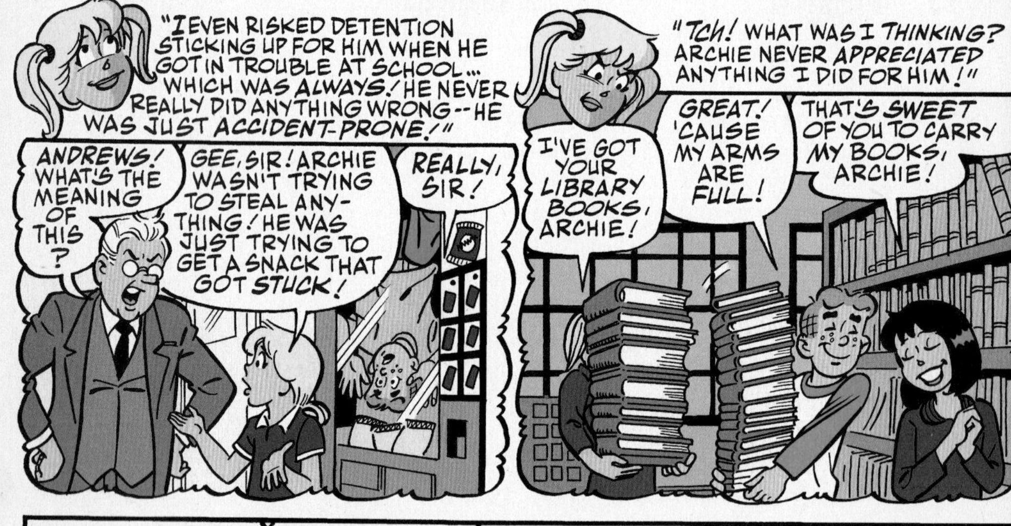
"I EVEN RISKED DETENTION STICKING UP FOR HIM WHEN HE GOT IN TROUBLE AT SCHOOL... WHICH WAS ALWAYS! HE NEVER REALLY DID ANYTHING WRONG--HE WAS JUST ACCIDENT-PRONE!"
ANDREWS! WHAT'S THE MEANING OF THIS?
GEE, SIR! ARCHIE WASN'T TRYING TO STEAL ANYTHING! HE WAS JUST TRYING TO GET A SNACK THAT GOT STUCK!
REALLY, SIR!
"TCH! WHAT WAS I THINKING? ARCHIE NEVER APPRECIATED ANYTHING I DID FOR HIM!"
I'VE GOT YOUR LIBRARY BOOKS, ARCHIE!
GREAT! 'CAUSE MY ARMS ARE FULL!
THAT'S SWEET OF YOU TO CARRY MY BOOKS, ARCHIE!

WHAT DID I EVER SEE IN THAT GUY? Ah, WELL--IT'S ALL IN THE PAST NOW--I'M OVER ARCHIE!
I'VE MATURED! AFTER ALL, I'M ENTERING NINTH GRADE! LET'S BE REAL! I'M PRACTICALLY A GROWN-UP NOW!
BETTY! THERE YOU ARE!
LOOK WHO I RAN INTO, DEAR!
Oh! HI, MRS. ANDREWS!
HELLO, BETTY! I'M HERE SHOPPING WITH ARCHIE! HE--
9

SAY! WHERE'D THAT BOY GO OFF TO--?
WHAT WAS THAT, DEAR?
PROBABLY SEEING IF RONNIE NEEDS HELP!
NOTHING, MOM!
AH-- I SEE HIM, BUT--
ARCHIE?
I TWISTED MY DARN ANKLE AND DROPPED MY PACKAGES! ARCHIE WAS SUCH A DEAR TO HELP ME!
NO PROB, MRS. DINKLEHOF! HEY, MRS. COOPER... HIYA, BETTY!
ARCHIE'S SO OBNOXIOUS!
FOOL-HARDY!
FICKLE!
I KNOW! I KNOW! BUT AT THE END OF THE DAY... HE'S SO SWEET!
ARCHIE, WHY DON'T YOU HELP MRS. DINKLEHOF OUT TO HER CAR? YOU CAN MEET US BACK HERE!
WHATEVER YOU SAY, MOM!
LET ME =OOF= HELP YOU, MRS. D.--!
WHAT A NICE BOY!
I'LL SAY!
SALE

SOON...
OKAY, NOW THAT I'VE DONE MY GOOD DEED FOR THE DAY, MAYBE I CAN GET MY SHOPPING DONE!
I HOPE BETTY STUCK AROUND... EVEN THOUGH IT'S TOUGH TO READ THAT GAL SOMETIMES! I CAN'T TELL IF SHE LIKES ME OR HATES MY GUTS!
Oh, WELL... FUNNY RUNNING INTO HER... EVERYONE'S HERE TRYING TO GET NEW STUFF BEFORE SCHOOL STARTS!

WELL, ALMOST EVERYONE... I THOUGHT I'D SEE JUGHEAD! NOW THAT I THINK OF IT, JUGGIE HASN'T EVEN MENTIONED ANYTHING ABOUT SCHOOL SUPPLIES OR NEW CLOTHES OR--
WELL! LOOK WHO IT IS!

IT'S JUGHEAD'S DAD! MAYBE JUGGIE'S WITH HIM--
HELLO, MR. JONES! I'VE GOT EVERYTHING READY FOR YOU!
GREAT!
Hmm! WHERE'S HE GOING?
POSTAL

WHAT'S MR. JONES DOING WITH ALL OF THOSE BOXES?
WE'LL MAKE SURE TO HOLD ANY MAIL FOR YOU AND YOUR FAMILY... AND WE'LL HAVE A TRUCK READY FOR YOU BY THE END OF THE WEEK!
THANKS!
MAIL? TRUCK? HEY-- WHAT'S GOING ON HERE?!
SEND IT TODAY!
THIS END UP

LATER, WHEN ARCHIE CATCHES UP WITH HIS MOM...
WHAT?
I SAID--MR. JONES GOT A NEW JOB--IN MONTANA!
P3
P2

MONTANA?!
YES-- THE JONESES ARE MOVING DURING THE LABOR DAY WEEKEND!

RIGHT BEFORE SCHOOL STARTS UP. DIDN'T JUGHEAD TELL YOU, DEAR?
NO.

BUT THIS EXPLAINS WHY HE'S BEEN ACTING SO ODD LATELY!
WELL... ODDER THAN USUAL! Chee-- MOVING!
Oh, HONEY! I KNOW YOU MUST BE DIS-APPOINTED!
MALL PARKING EXIT
RIVERDALE MALL

JUGHEAD IS YOUR BEST FRIEND AND HE'S MOVING AWAY. HE MUST BE VERY UPSET, TOO, IF HE DIDN'T SAY ANYTHING TO YOU! BUT ON THE UP-SIDE, DEAR, YOU'LL BE MAKING NEW FRIENDS AT A NEW SCHOOL!

AWESOME.

BEFORE LONG, THE LABOR DAY WEEKEND ARRIVES, AND MANY OF RIVERDALE'S FAMILIES GET TOGETHER FOR A PICNIC IN THE PARK...
SUMMER IS OVER! BOY, TIME FLIES!
Y'KNOW, PEOPLE USED TO COMPLAIN THAT NOTHING EVER CHANGES IN RIVERDALE --
--BUT ALL I'M SEEING IS CHANGE!
YEAH, THE KIDS ARE GROWING UP... STARTING HIGH SCHOOL...
GOOD FOLKS LIKE THE JONESES ARE MOVING AWAY... AND BAD EGGS ARE MOVING IN!
LIKE BIKERS!
THEY WOKE ME UP, TEARING AROUND ON THEIR MOTOR-CYCLES HALF THE NIGHT!
THAT NEVER HAPPENED IN OUR TOWN BEFORE!
I CAN'T BELIEVE THAT AFTER TODAY WE WON'T SEE YOU ANYMORE, JUG-HEAD!
CHIPS
WE'RE YOUR FRIENDS, JUG--WHY DIDN'T YOU TELL US YOU WERE MOVING?
I WAS HOPING IF I DIDN'T SAY ANY-THING...
...MAYBE IT JUST WOULDN'T HAPPEN!

THE KIDS ARE DOWN THAT THEIR FRIEND IS LEAVING RIVER-DALE!
AH, THEY'LL GET OVER IT! MY KID REGGIE IS LETTING IT ROLL OFF HIS BACK--
--YOU GOTTA TELL YOUR BOY TO MAN UP, ANDREWS!
WHAP
I THINK THE WRONG FAMILY'S LEAVING TOWN!
YOU THINK YOUR PROSPECTS ARE BETTER IN MONTANA THAN IN RIVER-DALE, JONES?
NOW, FRED!
WELL, HIRAM, I GOT A JOB OFFER THAT I COULDN'T RE-FUSE WITH A NEW COOK-WARE COMPANY!
THE OPPORTUNITY WAS TOO GOOD FOR FORSYTHE TO PASS UP! WE WERE CONCERNED ABOUT HOW THE YOUNGER FORSYTHE WOULD REACT TO LEAVING THE WORLD HE GREW UP IN...

...BUT HE'S HARDLY SAID A WORD ABOUT IT!
THAT'S BECAUSE WE JONESES ARE TROOPERS!
MORE POWER TO HIM--
ARCHIE IS CRUSHED! THEY'VE KNOWN EACH OTHER THEIR WHOLE LIVES!
OUR KIDS HAVE ALL KNOWN EACH OTHER THAT LONG!
I THINK THEY WERE ALL IN THE SAME PRE-SCHOOL CLASS...
YES, I RECALL THE FIRST TIME I SAW REGGIE'S NAME... IT WAS WRITTEN ON ARCHIE'S FORE-HEAD!
14

WITH ALL DUE RESPECT, MARY, YOUR BOY SEEMS TO ALWAYS GET UNDONE BY HIS OWN ANTICS!
NOW HOLD ON, HIRAM--!
FRED!

SEE HERE, LODGE--! I ADMIT ARCHIE CAN BE A, ER... HANDFUL AT TIMES... BUT WHAT TEENAGER ISN'T?!
MY VERONICA IS A LITTLE ANGEL--

--BUT THE ONLY TIME WE GOT CALLS FROM THE SCHOOL WAS WHEN SHE GOT INTO SOME PRE-DICAMENT BECAUSE OF ARCHIE!

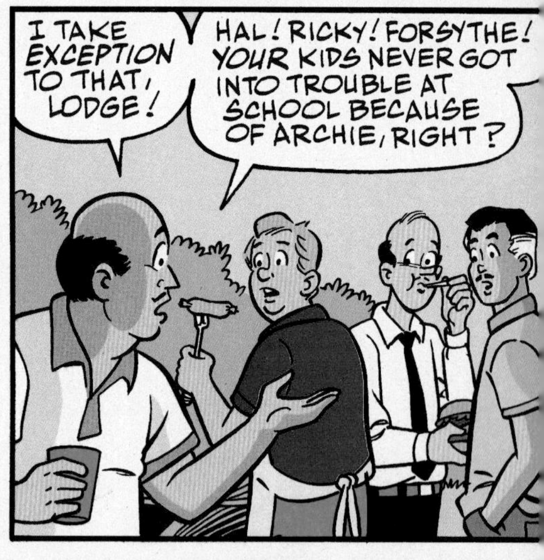
I TAKE EXCEPTION TO THAT, LODGE!
HAL! RICKY! FORSYTHE! YOUR KIDS NEVER GOT INTO TROUBLE AT SCHOOL BECAUSE OF ARCHIE, RIGHT?

RIGHT?

I NEED MORE WATER!
MAYBE WE SHOULD GET GOING, DEAR... WE HAVE A LONG TRIP AHEAD OF US!
KISS The COOK
15

ARCHIE'S A GOOD BOY! HE TENDS TO BE A VICTIM OF CIRCUMSTANCE MOST OF THE TIME!
REGGIE
ARCHIE UNFORTUNATELY GOT ON THE BAD SIDE OF THE PRINCIPAL OF THE MIDDLE SCHOOL--MR. WEATHERBEE WAS HIS NAME!
IT WAS ONE MIS-UNDERSTANDING AFTER ANOTHER!

AND ANOTHER, AND ANOTHER!
LET'S GO, HONEY... IT'S TIME TO LEAVE...
SO THIS IS IT, eh, JUG? I--
WELL, THAT IS--
AW, RELAX, ARCH... RE-LAAAX! WHAT'S DONE IS DONE! DON'T BE BUMMED...

I'LL BE BACK... YOU'LL SEE! LEMME GRAB ONE FOR THE ROAD AND I'M OUTTA HERE!
LATER, KIDS!
I--I CAN'T BELIEVE HE'S GOING!
I FEEL LIKE IT'S THE END OF AN ERA!
JUGGIE DIDN'T SEEM TOO BROKEN UP ABOUT LEAVING--!
AW, LET HIM GO! WHEN SCHOOL STARTS WE'LL GET A NEW SLACKER TO HANG WITH!
OKAY, OKAY! MAYBE OL' NEEDLENOSE WON'T BE SO EASY TO REPLACE! SHEESH!
17

AND SO ON THE LAST DAY OF VACATION... THE DAY BEFORE SCHOOL BEGINS...
THERE HE IS!
DIDN'T I TELL YOU HE'D BE HERE!?
OUT OF MY WAY!

HEY, BETTY--
DON'T "HEY BETTY" ME, ARCHIBALD ANDREWS! I'M SURPRISED AT YOU!

NOW WHAT DID I DO?!
YOUR BEST FRIEND IN THE WHOLE WORLD LEFT RIVERDALE!

THAT'S NOT EXACTLY BREAKING NEWS, BETTY! JUGGIE'S BEEN GONE FOR TWO DAYS!
YES! AND YOU HAVE NOT SHOWN THE SLIGHT-EST HINT THAT YOU MISS HIM!
BETTY'S GOT A POINT, ARCHIE-KINS! YOU'VE BEEN ACTING LIKE IT'S NO BIG DEAL!
BUT IT ISN'T!
GRR! HOW CAN YOU BE SO--SO--INDIFFERENT?! I EXPECT THIS ATTITUDE FROM REG, NOT YOU!
THERE'S HOPE FOR YOU YET, OLD MAN!
18

I TRY TO GIVE HIM THE BENEFIT OF THE DOUBT, BUT NOOOO!
I WARNED YOU ABOUT ANDREWS, GIRLS!
YOU WOULD EXPECT A BIT BETTER WHEN YOUR BEST FRIEND IS IN-VOLVED!
I'M REALLY SHOCKED!
HE'S A MEAN ONE, THAT ARCHIE ANDREWS IS!
SHEESH!

TWEET

THANK YOU! NOW THAT I HAVE YOUR ATTENTION, I'D LIKE YOU TO HEAR ME OUT!
PLEASE?

I'VE KNOWN JUGHEAD ALL MY LIFE--WE'VE BEEN THROUGH THICK AND THIN!
BUT WHEN I HEARD THOSE IMMORTAL WORDS--

--I KNEW SOMEHOW, SOME WAY--
--HE'LL FIND A WAY--
--JUGHEAD WILL GET THINGS UNDER CONTROL AND EVERY-THING IS GONNA BE OKAY!
WHAT IMMORTAL WORDS!?!
19

AW, RELAX, ARCH-- RELAAAX!
AND WHAT MAKES ME ABSOLUTELY SURE HE'LL BE BACK? --LOOK AT WHAT HE LEFT BEHIND AT MY HOUSE!

GASP!

THAT'S JUGGIE'S TACKY LITTLE CAP HE ALWAYS WEARS!
HE LOVES THAT DOPEY THING!
AND JUG WASN'T WEARING IT AT THE LABOR DAY PICNIC IN THE PARK!
EXACTLY! BECAUSE HE STASHED IT AT MY HOUSE, KNOWING FULL WELL THAT I'D FIND IT!
THAT'S WHY I'M NOT DOWN ABOUT JUG LEAVING! IF HE LEFT HIS MOST CHERISHED POSSESSION BEHIND...

...IT MUST BE HIS WAY OF SIGNALING TO US THAT HE'LL BE BACK FOR IT! AND IF JUG SAYS HE'LL BE BACK--
--MARK MY WORDS, HE WILL BE BACK!
THAT'S PRETTY WISHFUL THINKING--

--BUT OH, SO ADORABLE!
HE'S A LOYAL FRIEND! NAÏVE, BUT LOYAL!
YEESH! LOOK AT THEM SLOBBERING OVER HIM!
APOLOGY ACCEPTED!
20

Y'KNOW, ARCH, YOU CAN ALWAYS BE MY SIDEKICK!
I DON'T NEED MY SIDES KICKED, BUT THANKS ALL THE SAME!
MEH! JUST AS WELL! "GUILT BY ASSOCIATION" AND ALL THAT!

Oh, YEAH! HANG OUT WITH THIS GUY, AND YOU'LL EVENTUALLY BE DRAGGED INTO THE PRINCIPAL'S OFFICE!
THERE'S NO FLYING UNDER THE RADAR WITH ARCHIE!
!

WHOA, WHOA, WHOA!
FIRST OF ALL, THAT PRINCIPAL FROM OUR OLD SCHOOL HAD IT OUT FOR ME!

SECOND, TOMORROW REPRESENTS A FRESH START! ALL OF THAT "TROUBLE" IS BEHIND ME NOW!

I'LL BE KICKING OFF A NEW YEAR, AT A NEW SCHOOL WITH A CLEAN SLATE!
RIVERDALE HIGH SCHO

I'M REALLY LOOKING FORWARD TO IT!
BY YIMMINY! YOU HERE A DAY EARLY, HEY?

JUST WANTED TO CHECK OUT THE SCHOOL AND SET UP MY OFFICE SO I CAN PLUNGE INTO THE FIRST DAY OF SCHOOL--AND MY NEW JOB!
I'M SVENSON, THE CUSTODIAN. VELCOME ABOARD! YOU WILL LIKE IT HERE AT RIVERDALE HIGH, I BETCHA!
I'M SURE I VILL--I MEAN WILL! GOOD TO MEET YOU, SVENSON.
I'M WALDO WEATHERBEE, AND I'M PLEASED AS PUNCH TO BE YOUR SCHOOL'S NEW PRINCIPAL!
I'VE BEEN AN ADMINISTRATOR OF AN ELEMENTARY SCHOOL FOR QUITE SOME TIME... I WAS HAPPY TO HEAR I WAS BEING TRANSFERRED TO A HIGH SCHOOL!
BUT YER NEW STUDENTS VILL BE TEENAGERS, VEATHERBEE!
OH, I KNOW SOME ADOLESCENTS CAN BE DISRESPECTFUL AND UNRULY, BUT I'M PREPARED AFTER ALL I WENT THROUGH! YOU SEE, THERE WAS THIS CHILD IN GRADE SCHOOL, A RED-HEADED TROUBLE MAKER!
BOY, DID I HAVE MY HANDS FULL WITH THAT KID AND HIS ANTICS! THE STUNTS HE PULLED! THE SHENANIGANS I HAD TO ENDURE! LET ME TELL YOU--I HAD A FULL HEAD OF HAIR WHEN I STARTED THAT JOB!
THAT KID WAS A--A--

HRMPH! TUT-TUT! NEVER MIND THAT, SVENSON! TOMORROW REPRESENTS A FRESH START! ALL THAT "TROUBLE" IS BEHIND ME NOW!
VHATEVER YOU SAY, VEATHERBEE! VHATEVER YOU SAY!
END

RIVERDALE HIGH SCHOOL WAS ESTABLISHED IN 1941...
RIVERDALE HIGH
AND THROUGH THE YEARS, COUNTLESS STUDENTS HAVE ATTENDED THIS PILLAR OF LEARNING...
RIVERDALE HIGH
DESPITE CHANGING TRENDS, DIFFERENT FASHIONS, AND THE EVER-EVOLVING MOOD IN THE WORLD AROUND US...
GIVE A CHANCE
IF YOU CAN'T DIG IT, DON'T KNOCK IT!
RIVERDALE HIGH HAS BASICALLY REMAINED THE SAME PLACE IT'S ALWAYS BEEN... NO MATTER WHAT ERA!
RIVERDALE HIGH SCHOOL est. 1941
CASE IN POINT: ON THE DAY THE CURRENT GRADUATING CLASS ENTERED THE SCHOOL FOR THE FIRST TIME, IT WAS VERY APPARENT...
...THAT SOME THINGS NEVER CHANGE!
1

WRITER: *BATTON LASH* PENCILS: *BILL GALVAN*
INKS: *BOB SMITH* LETTERS: *JACK MORELLI* COLORS: *GLENN WHITMORE*
MANAGING EDITOR: *MIKE PELLERITO* EDITOR/EDITOR-IN-CHIEF: *VICTOR GORELICK*

MR. WEATHERBEE SAYS YOU CAN GO IN NOW.!
TH-THANKS!

AH, ARCHIE ANDREWS! COME IN, ANDREWS, COME IN! HAVE A SEAT!
YES, SIR!

WE GO BACK A WAYS, DON'T WE, ANDREWS? YOU KNOW WHAT WENT THROUGH MY MIND WHEN I SAW YOUR NAME AMONG THE STUDENT BODY?
I--I CAN IMAGINE...

IT BROUGHT BACK MANY FOND MEMORIES OF THE DAYS I WAS YOUR PRINCIPAL AT RIVERDALE ELEMENTARY SCHOOL!
FOND?

THAT'S GREAT! I AM SO RELIEVED TO HEAR THAT!
?!

ALL THIS TIME I THOUGHT YOU WERE ANGRY AT ME FOR OPENING THE FIRE HOSE BY ACCIDENT, OR FOR PUTTING BUBBLE BATH IN THE SCHOOL'S POOL, OR FOR THE TIME I GOT STUCK IN THE VENDING MACHINE, OR--

HEH! -- YOU WERE BEING SARCASTIC, WEREN'T YOU?

LOOK, ANDREWS-- THIS IS BOTH OUR FIRST DAY AT RIVERDALE HIGH. ME AS PRINCIPAL, AND YOU AS A STUDENT. DESPITE YOUR INAPPROPRIATE BEHAVIOR IN THE HALLWAY, I'M GOING TO LET YOU OFF WITH A WARNING...
BUT... THERE WAS A GANG OF...
I DON'T WANT TO HEAR ANY EXCUSES, ANDREWS! NO MORE ANTICS, UNDERSTAND? NOW GO TO CLASS!
RIGHT AWAY, SIR!
YES, SIR!
UNDERSTOOD, SIR!
AND THIS DAY STARTED OUT SO FINE!
GO BULLDOGS
"ME, RONNIE, BETTY -- EVEN REGGIE -- COULDN'T WAIT FOR SCHOOL TO START! WE WERE THERE BRIGHT AND EARLY...
R
"WE WERE ALL IN THE SAME HOMEROOM... BUT THERE WERE SO MANY KIDS I'D NEVER SEEN BEFORE!"
READ
4

"YEAH, I KNEW I WAS GOING TO LIKE IT HERE!"
RIVERDALE BULLDOGS
BULL DOGS

"UNTIL--!"
BUMP
OOF!

SORRY! I DIDN'T SEE YOU!
LOST YER WAY, FROSH?
YOU SHOULD WATCH WHERE YER GOIN', FROSH!
MEBBE JARED CAN HELP THIS FROSH!

WHERE YOU HEADING, FROSH?
I THINK I HAVE A MATH CLASS TO GET TO--

LEMME SEE... MEBBE I CAN HELP YOU FIND IT...
FOR A PRICE, THAT IS!
oh, boy.

"WHEN IT COMES TO BULLIES, I REMEMBERED MY FATHER'S ADVICE..."
JUST COUGH UP SOME DOUGH-- IT'S A FROSH TAX, KID!
SON, DON'T BE AFRAID OF A BULLY! STAND UP TO HIM... HE'S NOTHING BUT A COWARD!

LET'S GO, KID!
ARE YOU GONNA DIG FOR SOME CASH, OR DO WE HAFTA DIG IT OUT FOR YOU?
HOWEVER, IF YOU'RE UNFAIRLY OUTNUMBERED, THERE IS NO SHAME IN GETTING OUT OF THERE --AND FAST!

"DAD HAD GOOD ADVICE, BUT MAYBE I SHOULD'VE WATCHED WHERE I WAS GOING--!"
BUT THAT'S ALL BEHIND ME NOW! I CAUGHT A BREAK TODAY! I'LL BE OKAY IF I JUST GO TO MY CLASSES... STEER CLEAR OF THOSE BULLIES... AND KEEP OUT OF THE PRINCIPAL'S WAY...

MY NAME IS MS. GRUNDY, AND I HOPE THAT BY THE END OF THE SEMESTER YOU'LL FIND MATHEMATICS A FASCINATING SUBJECT...
MATHEMATICS
GERALDINE
GRUNDY

...BUT THAT MIGHT BE TOO "PI" IN THE SKY ON MY PART!
giggle!
MATHEMATICS
GERALDINE
GRUNDY
PSST! CARROT TOP! WHAT HAPPENED TODAY?
6

I HEARD McGERK DOESN'T LIKE YOU!
WHO DOESN'T LIKE ME?

JARED McGERK--HIM AND HIS BUDS ARE THE TOUGHEST KIDS IN SCHOOL...AND HE'S AFTER YOU, ARCH!
BUT I DIDN'T DO ANYTHING TO HIM!

WELL, McGERK AND HIS JERKS SAW YOU IN THE PRINCIPAL'S OFFICE SQUEALING ON THEM!
I WAS NOT! THEY GOT ME IN TROUBLE WITH THE PRINCIPAL!
I'LL TELL YOU ABOUT IT LATER, OKAY?

YOU HEARD FROM JUG YET?
NO.

WOULD NEEDLENOSE HAVE YOUR BACK, OR WOULD HE BE AS SCARED OF McGERK AND HIS JERKS AS YOU ARE?
GET SOME-THING STRAIGHT, REGGIE MANTLE--

JUGHEAD'S MY BEST FRIEND, AND I CAN ALWAYS COUNT ON HIM! AND IT WOULDN'T HAVE MATTERED IF JUG WAS THERE OR NOT!

I WAS NOT GETTING IN A FIGHT ON MY FIRST DAY OF HIGH SCHOOL! I'M ALREADY IN ENOUGH--

--TROUBLE.
7

WAIT UNTIL I GET MY HANDS ON REGGIE!
I LUCKED OUT THAT GRUNDY JUST SENT ME TO PICK UP BOOKS, AND NOT TO THE PRINCIPAL'S OFFICE--!
HEY, FROSH!
THERE'S A FROSH TOLL IN THIS HALLWAY, AND YOU HAFTA PAY TO GET THROUGH!
HAW! HAW!!
GROAN! NOT THEM AGAIN!
I DON'T CARE WHAT REGGIE THINKS! I'M NOT GOING FOUR AGAINST ONE!
I'LL TAKE THE LONG WAY BACK TO GRUNDY'S CLASS AND AVOID ANY TROUBLE!
WHUMP
MR. ANDREWS? THIS IS PRINCIPAL WEATHERBEE, RIVERDALE HIGH. I'D LIKE TO SEE YOU AND MRS. ANDREWS, REGARDING YOUR SON...
YES, IT DOES SEEM LIKE OLD TIMES...
UNFORTUNATELY!
THIS IS NOT HOW I IMAGINED MY FIRST DAY OF HIGH SCHOOL WOULD BE!
8

EVENTUALLY, THE FIRST DAY OF SCHOOL GIVES WAY TO THE SECOND, AND SO ON... AS EVERYONE SETTLES INTO THE FALL SEMESTER...
BIO
GYM
LIT
CLASSIC Literature
SOCIAL STUDIES
WORLD GEOGRAPHY
SIX WEEKS AFTER THE FIRST DAY...
I COULDN'T BELIEVE IT, DOUBLE A!
BURLEY'S NEARING DEATH, AND ONLY JULIA KNOWS HOW TO ADMINISTER HIS MEDICATION, BUT SHE'S NOT GOING TO HELP BECAUSE SHE'S IN CAHOOTS WITH YOU-KNOW-WHO--
--AT LEAST WE'RE LED TO THINK THAT! MEANWHILE, THERE'S A HIDDEN TUNNEL THAT PUTS DOC IN AN ETHICAL BIND, BUT HE--
9

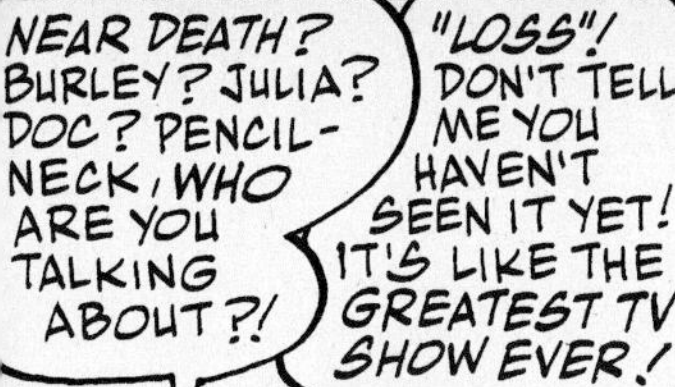
NEAR DEATH? BURLEY? JULIA? DOC? PENCIL-NECK, WHO ARE YOU TALKING ABOUT?!
"LOSS"! DON'T TELL ME YOU HAVEN'T SEEN IT YET! IT'S LIKE THE GREATEST TV SHOW EVER!

Oh, YEAH... IT'S A SERIAL, RIGHT? I THINK I MISSED TOO MUCH TO WATCH NOW, SO--
TOTALLY UNDER-STANDABLE, DOUBLE A! BUT I CAN LEND YOU THE FIRST FIVE SEASONS ON DVD! PROBLEM SOLVED!

THAT WON'T BE--
HEY! NO WORRIES, BRO! YOU CAN WATCH IT FROM THE BEGINNING, THEN WE CAN TALK ABOUT IT!

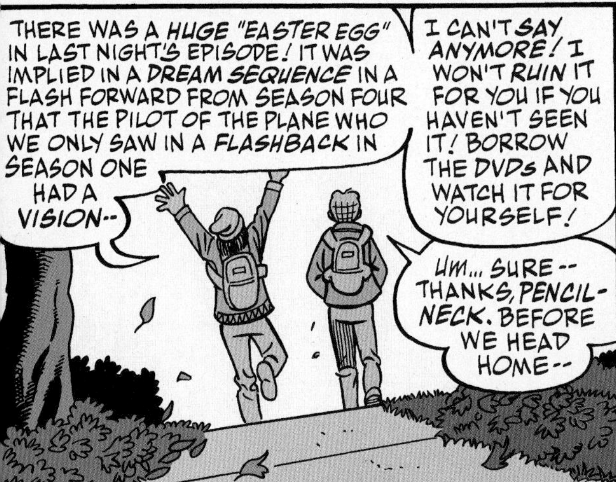
THERE WAS A HUGE "EASTER EGG" IN LAST NIGHT'S EPISODE! IT WAS IMPLIED IN A DREAM SEQUENCE IN A FLASH FORWARD FROM SEASON FOUR THAT THE PILOT OF THE PLANE WHO WE ONLY SAW IN A FLASHBACK IN SEASON ONE HAD A VISION--
I CAN'T SAY ANYMORE! I WON'T RUIN IT FOR YOU IF YOU HAVEN'T SEEN IT! BORROW THE DVDs AND WATCH IT FOR YOURSELF!
Um... SURE -- THANKS, PENCIL-NECK. BEFORE WE HEAD HOME--

--HOW ABOUT WE GRAB A BURGER?
Oooh... BURGERS MAKE ME QUEASY! I DON'T LIVE TO EAT, DOUBLE A-- I EAT TO LIVE!
HIDE, RONNIE!

Whew! WE ALMOST RAN INTO ANDREWS AND HIS JUGHEAD STAND-IN! I DON'T THINK IT'S WORKING OUT, THOUGH!
DON'T BE MEAN, REG! ARCHIE'S JUST BEING NICE! YOU COULD LEARN A THING OR TWO FROM HIM!

THEN LET'S GO OVER AND JOIN THEM, OKAY?
Ahhh... MAYBE ANOTHER TIME! I WAS HOPING WE COULD TRY OUT A NEW PLACE TO HANG OUT!
10

TH-THAT'S WHERE THE BIG KIDS HANG OUT, ISN'T IT?
YEAH. SO?
POP'S CHOCKLIT SHOPPE
AREN'T WE BIG KIDS NOW? WE'RE IN THE 9th GRADE! WE'VE GOT EVERY RIGHT TO BE HERE--

ONE WAY
EXIT

HEY! WHO LET THE LITTLE KIDS IN HERE?!

THAT PLACE IS TOO CLAUSTROPHOBIC! LET'S GO BACK ANOTHER TIME!
YEAH! LIKE WHEN WE'RE JUNIORS!!

LATER, AT THE ANDREWS' RESIDENCE...
Whew! PENCILNECK G IS AN OKAY GUY, BUT MAN, IS HE HYPER! I GUESS I'M USED TO JUGHEAD BEING SO LAID-BACK!
MOM? DAD? WHY ARE YOU LOOKING AT ME LIKE THAT? WHAT DID I DO NOW?
LOSS
LOSS
LOSS
A WHOLE DAY WENT BY AND THERE WAS NO CALL FROM THE PRINCIPAL, TEACHERS, OR ANY SCHOOL OFFICIAL! WHAT HAPPENED?!
SNACK SHORTA PLAGUES MONT
SHEESH! I CAN'T WIN AROUND HERE!
Oh, ARCHIE! YOUR FATHER'S TEASING! WE BOTH KNOW YOU HAVE A TENDENCY TO BE IN THE WRONG PLACE AT THE WRONG TIME!
LOSS
Sigh! WHAT-EVER!
BEFORE YOU GO, ARCHIE, I WANT TO SHOW YOU SOME-THING I PRINTED OUT...
I RECEIVED AN E-MAIL FROM GLADYS JONES TODAY, GIVING ME AN UPDATE ON HOW HER FAMILY IS DOING SINCE THEY MOVED TO MONTANA! SHE ATTACHED A PICTURE AND I THOUGHT YOU'D LIKE A COPY...
THANKS, MOM!
BEEF JERKY
12

I KNOW CHANGE IS A PART OF LIFE, BUT RIVERDALE IS JUST NOT THE SAME WITHOUT JUG!
OOPS! THERE GOES MY CELL!
THE SHIELD

HI, ARCH! MS. PACER IS LOOKING FOR FRESHMAN VOLUNTEERS TO WORK THE CONCESSION STAND AT THIS SATURDAY'S HOMECOMING DANCE! RONNIE AND REGGIE ARE IN... HOW ABOUT YOU?
IT'LL BE FUN!

AND DON'T WORRY--MS. PACER SAID COACH KLEATS IS WILLING TO FORGET THAT INCIDENT LAST WEEK!
OOOFFF!
THOOM
ARE YOU SURE? HE WAS AWFULLY SORE! HOW'D I KNOW THAT THE MACHINE WAS ON?
BEEP BEEP
HOLD ON, BETTY-- I HAVE AN-OTHER CALL!
5:00
DOUBLE A! I HAD AN IDEA-- I CAN COME OVER THIS SATURDAY AND WE CAN WATCH THE ENTIRE RUN OF "LOSS"!
DUDE--I KNOW I'VE SEEN THEM A MILLION TIMES, BUT I CAN ALWAYS FIND NEW "EASTER EGGS"!! WE CAN DO A MARATHON! I CAN ANNOTATE THE EPI-SODES WHILE WE WATCH! WOULDN'T THAT BE AWESOME?!
BETTY? COUNT ME IN!!
LOSS
LOSS
DOUBLE A? HELLO?
BLURP

AND ON SATURDAY...
WEATHERBEE IS LOOKING FOR YOU, PATTI!
I'LL BE RIGHT WITH HIM, COACH KLEATS!
I HAVE TO BE WITH THE FACULTY TO GREET A V.I.P., BUT I'M VERY HAPPY THAT YOU AND SAMIR HAVE VOLUNTEERED TO WORK THE CONCESSION STAND AT THE HOMECOMING DANCE, ARCHIE! GO JOIN THE OTHERS IN THE GYM... PLEASE ENTER THROUGH THE FRONT OR THE KITCHEN AREA... JUST STAY OUT OF THE CONTROL ROOM!
WELCOME BACK ALUMNI!!
WE'RE GOING TO HAVE A LIVE, CLOSED CIRCUIT BROADCAST OF THE BAND PLAYING AS THE ALUMNI GO FROM THE FIELD TO THE GYM! IT'S GOING TO BE WONDERFUL! THE TECHIES HAVE EVERYTHING WIRED UP AND READY TO ROLL...
YEAH! AND TRY NOT TO BOTCH IT, ANDREWS!
GOT A LITTLE HISTORY WITH COACH KLEATS?
IS IT THAT OBVIOUS? HEY! THERE'S REGGIE! HE'S SUPPOSED TO BE HELPING US OUT TODAY...
14

WHO'S THAT BIG KID HE'S TALKING TO?
HEY, REGGIE! OVER HERE!
GENTLEMEN! I'D LIKE YOU TO MEET MY MAN, MOOSE MASON!
HIYA!
REG! WE'VE GOT TO GET TO THE GYM! YOU COMING, OR WHAT?!
WHOA!
YOU DISRESPECTING MY FRIEND REGGIE?
CHILL, BIG GUY! LET ME HAVE A WORD WITH HIM FIRST!
MOOSE IS SOMETHING ELSE, Huh? I MADE FRIENDS WITH THE BIGGEST KID IN SCHOOL SO I WOULDN'T HAVE TROUBLE WITH BULLIES THE WAY YOU DO!
GOOD FOR YOU, REG.
THAT'S MY CELL! WHY DON'T YOU GUYS GO WITH SAMIR TO THE GYM? I'LL MEET YOU THERE!
HI, MOM. WHAT'S UP?
I WAS CALLING TO SAY YOUR FATHER AND I ARE RUNNING LATE BECAUSE :CRACKLE: AND :CRACKLE: ...WAIT TO SEE YOU! :CRACKLE:
MOM! BOY, THIS CON-NECTION IS BAD!
DID YOU HEAR ME, HONEY? :CRACKLE: ...WILL BE THERE! :BZZZZ: EXCITING?
WELL, YOU'D BETTER HURRY! THE HALFTIME SHOW IS ABOUT TO BEGIN!
:CRACKLE:
MOM? MOM?
15

WHAT WAS MOM TRYING TO TELL ME? Oh, WELL-- HER AND DAD WILL BE HERE SOON ENOUGH!

HEY! WHERE IS EVERYONE? WHAT'S THAT?
HELP! STOP! LEAVE US ALONE!

Oh, NO! McGERK AND HIS JERKS!
WASSAMATTER, BABY? TOO GOOD FOR ME?
FRANKLY, YES!

I'VE GOTTA CALL SECURITY!
GIT IN HERE!

NO ONE'S CALLIN' ANYONE! RIGHT, GUYS?!
R-RIGHT!
HAW! HAW!
8

REGGIE! WHAT HAPPENED TO MOOSE?!
FORGET HIM! ON THE WAY OVER HERE, THE BIG LUG SAW SOME CHICK IN THE STANDS!
"AND IT WAS ALL OVER FOR HIM!"
MIDGE! THAT GUY IS STARING AT YOU!
I'M SURE HE'S HARMLESS, NANCY! BESIDES, HE'S KINDA CUTE!

LOOKIE, LOOKIE, LOOKIE! IT'S THE FROSH!
TAXED, TOLLED, AND NOW TRAPPED!

MEAN-WHILE...
GLAD YOU COULD MAKE IT TO THE BIG HOMECOMING GAME, SUPERINTENDENT HAVERHILL!
HRMPH! AIR'S CHILLY!
PLEASE, SUPERINTENDENT-- TAKE MY BLANKET! I INSIST!
VERY WELL!
THE AIR'S NOT THE ONLY THING CHILLY!
I CAN'T TELL YOU, SUPER-INTENDENT, HOW MUCH I'VE ENJOYED BEING PRINCIPAL AT RIVERDALE HIGH!
WELL, DON'T GET USED TO IT, WEATHER-BEE!
YES, IT'S BEEN AN HONOR TO--
PARDON ME?
AS FAR AS I'M CONCERNED, YOU'RE HERE IN A TRIAL CAPACITY. FRANKLY, YOU MAY HAVE BEEN BETTER SUITED WITH YOUR OLD ELEMENTARY SCHOOL JOB...

B-BUT, SIR! I LOVE IT HERE!
WE'LL SEE, WEATHERBEE! WE'LL DISCUSS THIS ANOTHER TIME! IN THE MEANTIME, LET'S ENJOY THE GAME!

PERHAPS WE CAN WARM THE SUPERINTENDENT UP WITH SOME HOT SOUP? I CAN HAVE ARCHIE BRING UP--
PLEASE, MS. PACER... I'M ALREADY IN THE SOUP WITHOUT ANDREWS MAKING IT WORSE!

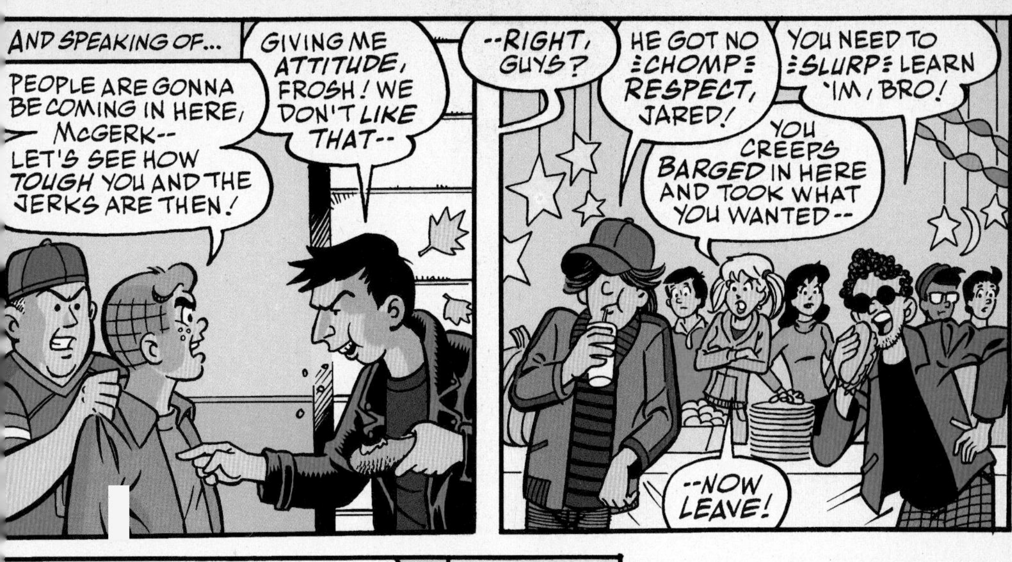
AND SPEAKING OF...
PEOPLE ARE GONNA BE COMING IN HERE, McGERK-- LET'S SEE HOW TOUGH YOU AND THE JERKS ARE THEN!
GIVING ME ATTITUDE, FROSH! WE DON'T LIKE THAT--
--RIGHT, GUYS?
HE GOT NO CHOMP RESPECT, JARED!
YOU NEED TO SLURP LEARN 'IM, BRO!
YOU CREEPS BARGED IN HERE AND TOOK WHAT YOU WANTED--
--NOW LEAVE!

I DIDN'T TAKE EVERYTHING I WANTED-- YOUR FRIEND THINKS SHE'S TOO GOOD FOR ME, BUT YOU, BLONDIE... HOWZABOUTIT?!
UGH!
COULDN'T RESIST THE ONIONS, HUH?
SUDDENLY...
GO GET HELP, ARCHIE!
I HEAR YA, FRANKIE!

BUT BEFORE ARCHIE COULD MAKE HIS MOVE...

YOU AIN'T GOIN' NOWHERE! I'M WARNING YOU-- I KNOW WHERE YOU ALL LIVE...

...AN' IF I HEAR THAT YOU SNITCHED ON ME AND MY BOYS, I SWEAR LIFE WILL BE MISERABLE FOR ALL OF YOU!!
KLIK
CAMERA ONE
18

AT THAT MOMENT...
I THINK YOU'RE READING TOO MUCH INTO HAVERHILL'S COMMENTS, MR. WEATHERBEE!
I DON'T HAVE TO READ ANYTHING, PACER! IT'S VERY CLEAR-- I'M FINISHED!
I WOULDN'T WORRY IF I WERE YOU, PRINCIPAL...
REALLY?
IT'S NOT PERSONAL... HAVERHILL HATED EVERY-ONE WHO HAD YOUR JOB! WHY SHOULD YOU BE DIFFERENT?

GROAN!
I'M DOOMED!
WHAT?

:sigh:... THIS HAS ALWAYS BEEN MY DREAM JOB! I HAD THE VISION FOR THE CURRICULUM... AND THE OPEN DOOR POLICY FOR ALL STUDENTS... EVEN A LOOSE CANNON LIKE--

--ANDREWS?!!
WELCOME BACK ALUMNI

AND TO SHOW YOU I MEAN BUSINESS, HERE'S SOMETHING TO REMEMBER ME BY...
GULP!
JUST MAKE IT QUICK!

PUT THAT BOY DOWN!
LET GO, PUNK!!

GOTTA GET OUT THE WAY I SNUCK IN... THROUGH THE KITCHEN!

SLAM
REGGIE!

REG! SORRY I TOOK SO LONG, BUT I MET THE MOST BEE-YOO-TEE-FUL GIRL...

HER NAME IS MIDGE, AND SHE -- HEY, REG! YOU OKAY?
REGGIE HAD A ROUGH DAY!
REGGIE HAD A ROUGH DAY?

DID THAT DELINQUENT HURT YOU, ARCHIE? ARE YOU ALL RIGHT?
GEE, MR. WEATHERBEE -- YOU'RE SO CONCERNED! ARE YOU SURE YOU'RE ALL RIGHT!?
ARCHIE!!
MOM! DAD!!
WE ARRIVED AND SAW YOU ON THE BIG SCREEN! AT FIRST WE THOUGHT IT WAS A GAG!
WE WERE WORRIED! ARE YOU HURT, BABY?!
MAAA--! I'M FINE!
I KNEW I SHOULD'VE SENT YOU TO PRIVATE SCHOOL!
OH, DADDYKINS! THERE'S MORE ADVENTURE TO BE FOUND HERE WITH THE HOI POLLOI!
IT WAS CLEVER OF YOU KIDS TO USE THE FIELD'S CLOSED CURCUIT MONITOR AS A WAY TO CALL FOR HELP!
BUT, DADDY -- WE WEREN'T ANYWHERE NEAR THE CONTROL ROOM!
THEN WHO--?

JUGHEAD!
HELLO, THERE!
21

YOU'RE BACK!
I CAN'T BELIEVE YOU'RE HERE, BUDDY!
HOW DID YOU GET IN THE CONTROL BOOTH?
I WANTED TO SURPRISE YOU! YOUR MOM TOLD ME YOU'D BE IN THE GYM!
"I CAME THROUGH THE KITCHEN AND SAW THE TROUBLE! I DIDN'T HAVE MY CELL PHONE, THOUGH...
CHIPS
"WHILE THOSE GOONS WERE DISTRACTED, I SNUCK INTO THE CONTROL ROOM TO USE A MICROPHONE TO CALL FOR HELP... I DIDN'T REALIZE I SWITCHED ON A CAMERA-THINGY!"
WHAT'S THE DIFFERENCE? YOU SAVED THE DAY!
HEY! WATCH IT, COOPER!
BUT, JUG! WHAT ARE YOU DOING IN RIVERDALE? I THOUGHT YOU WERE SETTLED IN MONTANA BY NOW!
AFTER THREE MONTHS IN THE MOUNTAINS, MY ASTHMA COULDN'T TAKE THE THIN AIR! BESIDES, OUR HEART WASN'T IN MONTANA...
...IT WAS HERE IN RIVERDALE!
THAT'S WHY YOUR FATHER AND I WERE LATE TO THE GAME! YOU COULD'VE KNOCKED US OVER WITH A FEATHER WHEN WE SAW THE JONESES AT OUR DOOR!
22

I KNEW I WOULD'VE RUINED JUGHEAD'S SURPRISE, BUT I COULDN'T RESIST TELLING YOU!
THAT'S WHAT YOU WERE TRYING TO SAY ON THE PHONE!
SO THAT'S THE FAMOUS JUGHEAD YOU'VE BEEN TALKING ABOUT!
WAIT'LL PENCIL-NECK G MEETS HIS RIVAL!
OMIGOSH! WE STILL HAVE TO GET READY FOR THE HOME-COMING DANCE!
WHERE'S JUGHEAD? I WANT TO SHAKE HIS HAND!
YEAH--! WHERE'D HE GO? WE'VE GOT TO TELL HIM ALL ABOUT RIVERDALE HIGH--!

I'M LISTENING! I'M LISTENING! HEROICS CAN GIVE A GUY AN APPETITE!

MEANWHILE, OUTSIDE...
HRMPH! THOSE BOYS HAVE APPARENTLY BEEN A PROBLEM AT RIVERDALE FOR SOME TIME!
WEATHERBEE EXPELLED THEM ON THE SPOT! THEY WON'T BE A BLIGHT ON THE SCHOOL ANYMORE, SIR!
RIVERDAL
POLIC

STILL. THERE ARE MANY THINGS ABOUT THIS SCHOOL THAT I HAVE LONG THOUGHT LEFT A LOT TO BE DESIRED! AND I DOUBT WEATHER-BEE IS UP TO THE TASK!
YOU'LL FIND OUT, SUPERINTENDENT HAVERHILL. I'LL BE YOUR EYES AND EARS!

YES, INDEED! NO ONE WILL KNOW YOU WORK FOR ME. AS FAR AS ANYONE'S CONCERNED, YOU'VE TRANSFERRED HERE FROM ANOTHER DISTRICT. YOU'LL BE AT RIVERDALE HIGH DAY IN, DAY OUT TO SEE FIRST HAND WHAT REALLY GOES ON THERE!
YES...NEXT TERM WILL TELL THE TALE!
END

VROOM VROOM
RIVERDALE HAS ALWAYS BEEN A NICE PLACE TO LIVE...
... AND WE'D LIKE TO KEEP IT THAT WAY!!
ONE WAY
RIVERDALE SCHOOL DISTRICT

WE HAVE REVIEWED THE REPORTS OF MR. WEATHERBEE AND THE PRINCIPAL WHO PRECEEDED HIM CONCERNING YOUR CONDUCT AT RIVERDALE HIGH...

... JARED McGERK, NOT ONLY DOES YOUR CUMULATIVE EDUCATIONAL RECORD LEAVE MUCH TO BE DESIRED--

--BUT YOUR CONTINUED PRESENCE IN RIVERDALE HIGH POSES A THREAT TO THE OTHER STUDENTS.

THIS SCHOOL BOARD REJECTS YOUR APPEAL TO BEING EXPELLED. YOUR EXPULSION STANDS.
DO YOU HAVE ANYTHING TO SAY, YOUNG MAN?

YEAH... TELL ANDREWS I'LL BE IN TOUCH...
1

FRESHMAN YEAR

PART 3 OF 5

WRITER: *BATTON LASH* PENCILS: *BILL GALVAN*
INKS: *BOB SMITH* LETTERS: *JACK MORELLI*
COLORS: *GLENN WHITMORE*
MANAGING EDITOR: *MIKE PELLERITO*
EDITOR/EDITOR-IN-CHIEF: *VICTOR GORELICK*

WATCH OUT FOR THE ICE, ARCH.
THANKS FOR THE HEADS-UP, PAL...
WHAT WAS I SAYING?

RONNIE.
YEAH! I THINK SHE REALLY LIKES ME. I BEGAN LEAVING LITTLE "STICKY" NOTES ON HER HOMEROOM DESK AS A GOOF...

...AND SHE BEGAN TO LEAVE ME LITTLE NOTES IN RETURN!
uh-huh.
"I WAS LOOKING FORWARD TO EVERY CLASS TO SEE IF RONNIE WOULD LEAVE A LITTLE "STICKY NOTE" FOR ME! AND I'D SURPRISE HER WITH ONE... IT WAS SO MUCH FUN!"
PEEK A-BOO! AA
Where were you today? Miss you! V.L.

BUT THEN WE HAD SCHOOL OFF FOR THE HOLIDAYS, AND RONNIE SPENT CHRISTMAS IN EUROPE, SO I WASN'T ABLE TO SEE HER...
IN HERE.
TRUE, I WAS DISAPPOINTED WHEN I DIDN'T GET AN E-MAIL FROM HER DURING THE ENTIRE VACATION, BUT MAYBE HER FATHER WOULDN'T ALLOW HER TO CONTACT ME. SHEESH, THAT GUY CAN HOLD A GRUDGE!
Ah! MR. JONES!
3

STILL, RONNIE DID SEND A "WISH YOU WERE HERE" CARD... I TOOK THAT AS A GOOD SIGN...
I HAVE YOUR ITEM READY, SIR!
COOL!
I'M CURIOUS TO SEE IF RONNIE WILL LEAVE ME A NOTE FIRST, OR WAIT FOR ME TO LEAVE ONE FOR HER ONCE SCHOOL RESUMES...
HEY!
WHAT'RE WE DOING IN A HAT STORE?

I DON'T KNOW WHERE YOU KEPT MY CAP WHILE I WAS AWAY, ARCH, BUT IT SORELY NEEDED TO BE CLEANED AND BLOCKED!
EXCELLENT JOB, MY GOOD MAN!
THENKEW!
WELL, EXCUUUSE ME! I THOUGHT I WAS DOING YOU A FAVOR!
AW, I'M JUST BUSTIN' ON YA, ARCH! YOU KNOW I WOULDN'T HAVE JUST ANYONE MIND THE OL' CHAPEAU!
Ahem, SIR?

THERE'S A MATTER FOR SERVICES RENDERED!
Hmm... THAT'S A BIT STEEPER THAN I THOUGHT! ARCH?
BILL
YOU'RE LUCKY I HAD CASH ON ME! I OUGHTA CHARGE YOU FOR STORING THAT CAP WHILE YOU WERE GONE!
AW, RELAX, ARCH! THANKS FOR THE LOAN... I'LL PAY YOU BACK AT MY HOUSE! AND IF YOU WANT, I'LL EVEN LEAVE VERONICA A "STICKY NOTE" TELLING HER WHAT A GREAT GUY YOU ARE... AND GENEROUS, TOO!
4

AND SO, IN CONCLUSION, AS WE PREPARE FOR THE START OF A NEW TERM MONDAY...
YEESH! WALDO'S BEEN CONCLUDING FOR OVER AN HOUR!
I ADMIT HE'S LONG WINDED, GERALDINE, BUT HE DOES MAKE AN EFFORT TO WORK WITH THE FACULTY...
...UNLIKE HIS PREDECESSORS!
I'D LIKE TO THANK YOU ALL FOR COMING IN A DAY EARLY TO REVIEW THE AGENDA FOR THE NEW TERM.
RIVERDALE HIGH SCHOOL
BUT BEFORE WE ADJOURN, I'D LIKE TO WELCOME THE NEW ADDITIONS TO THE RIVERDALE HIGH FACULTY! PLEASE STAND WHEN I SAY YOUR NAME.
BILL NEE, WHO WILL JOIN THE HISTORY DEPARTMENT.
HELLO.
JACKIE FLORES, WHO WILL TEACH COMPUTERS AND TELECOMMUNICATIONS.
HI!
AND SAM BURROWS, WHO TRANSFERRED HERE FROM CENTRAL HIGH.
HEY!
YOU'LL LIKE RIVERDALE HIGH, BUDDY. IT'S NICE HERE. I HEAR CENTRAL HIGH IS A PRETTY ROUGH SCHOOL!
UM, YEAH, SURE! I GUESS SO!
WELCOME ABOARD TO OUR NEW TEACHERS, AND WELCOME BACK TO EVERYONE ELSE! BUT BEFORE WE WRAP IT UP, LET ME JUST SAY--
YIMMINY, SVENSON! VEN IS HE GONNA FINISH UP?
NOW, NOW, GREGER! YOU NEW HERE... YOU SEE DAT VEDDERBEE IS GOOD EGG... LONG VINDED, BOT GOOD EGG!
5

AFTER NOT HEARING FROM HER FOR THE WHOLE HOLIDAY BREAK, I WAS GLAD RONNIE TEXT MESSAGED ME THAT SHE NEEDS ME TO COME OVER TONIGHT!

NEEDS ME, eh? THE POOR THING MUST'VE REALLY MISSED ME. I JUST HOPE HER FATHER ISN'T STILL ANGRY ABOUT ME--
DING DONG

Uh, HI! I'M HERE TO SEE VERONICA.
Oh, IT'S YOU.
LET HIM IN, SMITHERS.

H-HI, MR. LODGE! I GOT A MESSAGE FROM RONNIE, AND...
YES! YES! I KNOW! SHE'S WAITING FOR YOU!

THIS WAY, MY BOY! LET ME ESCORT YOU!
GEE, THANKS, MR. LODGE! HOW WAS YOUR EUROPEAN VACATION?
6

Oh, EXCELLENT! IT WAS WHAT THE DOCTOR ORDERED --LITERALLY, AFTER THE NEAR-BREAKDOWN I HAD BEFORE THE HOLIDAYS!
NEAR COUGH BREAK-DOWN, SIR?

YES! BUT DON'T WORRY! I GOT OVER IT! I ADMIT I WAS A TAD UPSET TO SEE MY PRICELESS YOSHIDA VASE, WITH ITS EXQUISITE CALLIGRAPHY, RUINED BY SOME BLOCKHEAD!

BUT WITH THE CARE OF MY LOVING FAMILY, AND RELAXING IN THE FRENCH ALPS, I WAS ABLE TO TAKE A MORE... POSITIVE OUTLOOK!
I'M REALLY SORRY ABOUT THAT VASE, SIR--!

I HAD NO IDEA WHEN I SLID DOWN THAT BANNISTER, I'D GO FLYING ACROSS THE ROOM AND KNOCK IT OVER!
I DID TRY TO FIX IT, SIR!
THAT YOU DID, LAD! YOU KNOW, I HAD TOLD VERONICA THAT I NEVER WANTED YOU IN MY HOUSE AGAIN...

BUT SHE PERSISTED, AND WE COMPROMISED! SHE PROMISED ME YOU WON'T BE LEFT TO YOUR OWN DEVICES ANYMORE!
Oh, NO!

RONNIE ASSURED ME SHE'LL ONLY INVITE YOU OVER WHEN THERE ARE PLENTY OF OTHER PEOPLE AROUND...
MAYBE THEY'LL STOP YOU BEFORE YOU DO ANY FURTHER DAMAGE TO MY PROPERTY!
ARCHIEKINS!! YOU MADE IT!!
7

ENJOY YOUR-SELF, KIDS!
RONNIE! WHEN YOU MESSAGED ME, I THOUGHT YOU-- I MEAN WE-- I--!
Oh, ARCHIEKINS! I MEANT WHAT I WROTE -- I DO NEED YOU!
WE'RE ALL NEEDED TO HELP THE RIVER-DALE HIGH DRAMATIC ARTS PLAYERS!
YO, YO, YO, CARROT-TOP!

I SAW A BULLETIN ON THE SCHOOL'S WEBSITE ASKING FOR STUDENTS TO HELP WITH THE SCHOOL PLAY!
SO I E-MAILED MS. LOVETT, THE DRAMA TEACHER, THAT I WOULD COORDINATE THE VOLUNTEERS!
I CAN HELP WITH PROPS AND COS-TUMES!
ME, MIKE AND VICTOR CAN HANDLE THE HEAVY LIFTING AND SCENERY CHANG-ING!
I'LL HELP PAINT THE BACK-DROPS!

AND WHAT'S YOUR CONTRIBUTION, REGGIE?
I'M HERE FOR THE CULTURE... AND CHICKS LOVE CULTURE!
NUTS! I WAS HOPING IT WOULD BE JUST ME AND RONNIE! I DON'T WANNA BE ONE OF HER STAGE-HANDS!
BETTY COOPER HERE TO SEE YOU, MISS VERONICA.
Ah! BETS GOT MY MESSAGE! I HAVEN'T SEEN HER SINCE--
8

--H-H-HOLIDAYS?
HI, EVERYONE! SORRY I'M LATE!
BETTY! IS THAT YOU?!

WOW! YOU LOOK GREAT!
Oh, THANK YOU! BUT IT'S MY BEST BUD WHO I HAVE TO THANK!
Y-YOU DO?
FOR CHRISTMAS, RONNIE GAVE ME A GIFT CERTIFICATE FOR THE BEST SPA IN TOWN! I GOT A COMPLETE MAKE-OVER! -- FACIAL, HAIR, NAILS -- THE WORKS!
!
10

ALL IN TIME FOR A NEW TERM! RONNIE, YOU'RE THE BEST FRIEND ANYONE COULD ASK FOR! SO WHATEVER YOU NEED, I'M HERE FOR YOU!
Oh, WE HAVE PLENTY OF VOLUNTEERS, SO THERE'S NO NEED FOR YOU TO --
HEY, BETTY--
I GUESS WE'LL BE WORKING ALONGSIDE AS STAGE-HANDS--
ONE SIDE, ANDREWS! YOU'RE NOT THE ONLY VOLUNTEER HERE!
YOU'RE A GOOD PERSON TO GIVE THAT MAKE-OVER TO BETTY! IT MUST'VE BEEN VERY EXPENSIVE!
YEAH, I CAN'T AFFORD TO BE SO GOOD!
9

AND SO, AS THE NEW TERM BEGINS...
BRRIIIINNGG
WELCOME BACK, CLASS! I HOPE YOU ENJOYED YOUR MINI-VACATION, BUT NOW IT'S BACK TO WORK. OPEN UP YOUR HISTORY BOOKS--
RIVERDALE HIGH SCHOOL
EST. 1941

--WE'RE GOING TO LOOK AT THE LIVES OF SEVERAL WOMEN OF DISTINCTION...
YEAH... DISTINCTION!!
HISTORY IN THE MAKING...
10

SIGH! I'M SO LUCKY TO HAVE TWO FABULOUS BABES IN MY LIFE! BUT WHO DO I CHOOSE? AH, THAT'S ONE FOR THE BOOKS!
VERONICA EARHART! WAIT! DON'T YOU KNOW YOU'RE FLYING OVER UNCHARTED TERRITORY?
I'M NOT AFRAID, ARCHIEKINS! COME WITH ME--AND WE CAN GET LOST TOGETHER!
I DUB THEE SIR ARCHIBALD ANDREWS!
I AM INDEED HONORED, QUEEN ELIZABETH!
OH, PLEASE! I'M NOT ONE TO STAND ON CEREMONY! CALL ME QUEEN BETTY--!
LET'S GO GRAB A SODA!
WUPPA WUPPA WUPPA
WHAT'S THAT!?
11

LET'S GO FOR A RIDE IN MY PERSONAL CHOPPER, ARCHIEKINS!
YOU HAVE YOUR OWN HELICOPTER? COOL!
ARCHIE ANDREWS! IS THIS HOW YOU TREAT ALL YOUR SUBJECTS!?
MY SUBJECTS? YOU'RE THE QUEEN!!
WHATEVER!-- AS LONG AS YOU KNOW WHO'S IN CHARGE!
I ASKED YOU IF YOU DAYDREAM LIKE THIS IN ALL YOUR SUBJECTS OR JUST IN MY HISTORY CLASS?
HAHA HAHA HAHA
ULP!
NOW, THEN, MR. ANDREWS -- CAN YOU NAME AT LEAST TWO WOMEN OF DISTINCTION THAT WE'VE BEEN DISCUSSING--?
ER...
BETTY AND VERONICA?
12

SHEESH! I WON'T LIVE THAT DOWN FOR A WHILE! THE CLASS SURE HAD A GOOD OLD TIME AT MY EXPENSE! AWW... IT'LL PASS...

AT LEAST I DON'T HAVE TO WORRY ABOUT BULLIES HARASSING ME! NOW THAT McGERK'S BEEN EXPELLED, IT'S BEEN SAFE TO--
ARCHIE ANDREWS?

YOW!
I GOTTA TALK TO YOU--

--I NEED YOUR HELP!

ELSE-WHERE...
I THINK IT'S JUST SUPER WHEN FRESHMEN WANT TO GET INVOLVED IN SCHOOL ACTIVITIES...
POP'S

...VERONICA, YOU'VE DONE AN AMAZING JOB ORGAN-IZING YOUR CLASSMATES FOR THE DRAMA CLASS!
MY PARENTS HAVE ALWAYS BEEN PATRONS OF THE ARTS! I GUESS I INHERITED MY INTEREST FROM THEM!
13

AH! THERE ARE OUR THESPIANS NOW! I'LL BRING THEM OVER!
WE'LL BE RIGHT HERE, MS. LOVETT!
AH-HA! NOW I SEE THE METHOD TO YOUR MADNESS, MISS "PATRON OF THE ARTS"!
WHATEVER DO YOU MEAN, REGINALD?

THE DRAMA CLASS HANGS OUT HERE AT THE CHOCKLIT SHOP! IF WE'RE IN WITH THEM, WE'RE IN WITH POP'S!
GOSH! WHAT A COINCIDENCE! BUT YOU ARE CORRECT, SIR!
VERONICA, REGGIE, I'D LIKE YOU TO MEET THE RIVERDALE HIGH DRAMATIC ARTS PLAYERS!
HEY, POP! YOU LETTIN' LITTLE KIDS HANG OUT IN HERE, NOW?
BUT WE'VE A LONG WAY TO GO!

MEANWHILE...
IT'S AS SIMPLE AS THAT! I'M WILD ABOUT MIDGE KLUMP -- BUT SHE DOESN'T KNOW I'M ALIVE! SHE'S AN ARTIST-- AND SMART! I'M JUST A BIG LUG!
I FEEL FOR YOU, MOOSE, BUT WHAT CAN I DO?
I WAS HOPING YOU COULD GIVE ME SOME ADVICE! YOU'VE GOT A WAY WITH THE LADIES!
I DO, DON'T I...?
14

I GUESS I'M BLESSED WITH THE CULT OF PERSONALITY! BUT CAN I GIVE YOU A TIP?
SURE! SURE! ANY-THING!
WELL, THE WAY I GOT CLOSER TO VERONICA WAS BY LEAVING "STICKY NOTES" ON HER DESKS AND LOCKERS. THEY WERE JUST SILLY LITTLE NOTES TO MAKE HER LAUGH AND GET HER THROUGH THE DAY!
YEAH?
THE TRICK IS TO KEEP IT LIGHT. DON'T GO HEAVY ON THE MUSHY STUFF. VERONICA LOOKED FORWARD EVERY DAY TO SEE WHAT KOOKY NOTE I WAS GOING TO LEAVE. I BET MIDGE WOULD FEEL THE SAME WAY!
ARCH! YOU'RE A GENIUS!
A FEW DAYS LATER...
I NEED ELOQUENCE, AND I HAVE NONE!
I'LL LEND YOU MINE!
SCRIPT
LEND ME YOUR CONQUERING PHYSICAL CHARM, AND TOGETHER WE'LL FORM A ROMANTIC HERO!
HOW WAS THAT, MS. LOVETT?
SORRY, FELLAHS, I WAS DISTRACTED!
MAN! I NEVER KNEW HOW MUCH WORK WENT INTO PUTTING ON A PLAY!
RIVERDALE HIGH DRAMATIC ARTS PLAYERS — PRESENTS — CYRANO DE BERGERAC

I'VE GOT A TON OF HOMEWORK, SO I CAN'T REALLY STAY TOO LONG AFTER SCHOOL. I NEED MOST OF MY TIME--
WELL, YOU CAN HELP ME WITH PASTING UP THAT SPOT UP THERE--

VERONICA! THOSE CHATTERING STUDENTS ARE VERY DISTRACTING! CAN YOU DO ME A FAVOR AND BREAK THEM UP!?
GLADLY, MS. LOVETT!

WILL YOU TWO KEEP IT DOWN?? YOU'RE DISRESPECTING THE PERFORMERS!
OUR BAD, RONNIE! WE'LL BE ON OUR BEST--
OOPS!

VERONICA! WHAT CAN I DO TO MAKE AMENDS?
--BEHAVIOR?
Hmmm... LET ME THINK...

YOU COULD HELP ME MOVE SOME COSTUME RACKS...
I'M THERE!
AND RUN TO THE CRAFT STORE FOR SUPPLIES...
YOU GOT IT!
MAYBE YOU CAN GET ME A BOTTLE OF SPRING WATER-- THE CARBONATED DRINKS IN THE SCHOOL VENDING MACHINES JUST WON'T DO!
I'M AT YOUR DISPOSAL!
NO KIDDING! GROAN!
16

MEANWHILE THE STUDENTS AREN'T THE ONLY ONES FACING NEW HORIZONS THIS SEMESTER...
WHAT DO YOU THINK OF MY PROPOSAL, WALDO?
IT'S AN INTERESTING IDEA... BUT--
IT'S THE PERFECT COLLABORATION OF TWO DEPARTMENTS! "PRIMITIVE CAVE PAINTINGS"! THE STUDENTS CAN STUDY THEM IN HISTORY, AND MAKE THEM IN ART!
YES, BUT IT WOULD BE A SCHEDULING NIGHTMARE! AND FRANKLY, BILL, YOU ARE TOO NEW TO THE FACULTY TO BE SUGGESTING NEW ELECTIVES! PARTICULARLY ONE SO SPECIALIZED!
PROPOSALS

BUT THIS COULD BE A GROUND-BREAKING PROGRAM!
PERHAPS. BUT FOR NOW, THE SCHOOL DOESN'T HAVE THE RESOURCES FOR SUCH AN ENDEAVOR!

NOW, IF THERE'S NOTHING FURTHER...
THANK YOU FOR YOUR TIME.
?

I HOPE I DIDN'T INTRUDE...
NOT AT ALL, SAM... YOU ARRIVED JUST IN TIME...

...THAT BUSINESS WITH MR. NEE IS FINISHED.
AND SO, THE NEW TERM GETS UNDERWAY...
17

AS DAYS TURN INTO WEEKS LEADING UP TO "OPENING NIGHT"...
I WAS AFRAID THAT SCHOOL PLAY WOULD BE TOO DEMANDING OF ARCHIE'S TIME, AND INTERFERE WITH HIS SCHOOLWORK...
BUT IT WAS NICE OF BETTY TO OFFER TO HELP WITH HIS STUDIES!
I WOULD'VE FORGOTTEN TOMORROW'S MATH TEST IF YOU HADN'T REMINDED ME, BETTY!
DON'T MENTION IT, ARCHIE!
ANOTHER "STICKY NOTE", MIDGE? HOW LONG HAVE YOU BEEN GETTING THEM?
EVERY DAY FOR ALMOST TWO WEEKS, NANCY!
THEY WERE CUTE--AT FIRST. I'M NOT SURE IF I SHOULD TRY AND APPROACH HIM...
EVEN THOUGH I'M NOT HELPING WITH THE PRODUCTION, I CAN'T RESIST A LITTLE TREAT FROM THIS FINE SPREAD...
JUGHEAD JONES!
FOR CAST AND CREW ONLY!
BUSTED! Chomp!
Hmmm... I DIDN'T NOTICE THIS BEFORE... TELL YOU WHAT, MR. JONES... YOU CAN EARN THAT TREAT! COME WITH ME!
IF YOU CAN MOLD THE PROSTHETIC TO RESEMBLE JUGHEAD'S NOSE, WE MIGHT HAVE A CYRANO THAT KEEPS WITH TRADITION, BUT WITH A CONTEMPORARY FLARE!
JUGGIE! YOU'RE NOT INSULTED?
NOT WITH THESE PERKS!
18

THANKS FOR WALKING ME HOME, ARCHIE!
IT'S THE LEAST I CAN DO, AFTER ALL THE HELP YOU'VE BEEN, BETS-- HEY!
LOOK WHO'S HANGING OUT AT POP'S WITH THE JUNIORS! VERONICA'S PRETTY COOL, EH?
WHATEVER!
FINALLY, THE BIG NIGHT ARRIVES...
CYRANO DE BERGERAC by EDMOND ROSTAND
The RIVERDALE HIGH DRAMATIC ARTS PLAYERS PRESENTATION
WELCOME TO THE RIVERDALE HIGH DRAMATIC ARTS PLAYERS' PRESENTATION OF EDMOND ROSTAND'S CLASSIC PLAY-- "CYRANO DE BERGERAC"! AS PRINCIPAL OF THIS FINE SCHOOL--
--I'M PLEASED TO INTRODUCE TO YOU--

--ER... THE CHAIR OF THE DRAMA DEPARTMENT... SAMANTHA LOVETT!
THANK YOU, PRINCIPAL WEATHER-BEE!
CLAP CLAP CLAP CLAP CLAP

YOU GET A BAD CASE OF STAGE FRIGHT, VEDDERBEE?
NO, SVENSON -- I GOT UNNERVED WHEN I SAW SUPERINTENDENT HAVERHILL IN THE AUDIENCE!

WHY IS HE HERE? IS HE CHECKING UP ON ME??
HEY, YOU GUYS! KEEP IT DOWN!

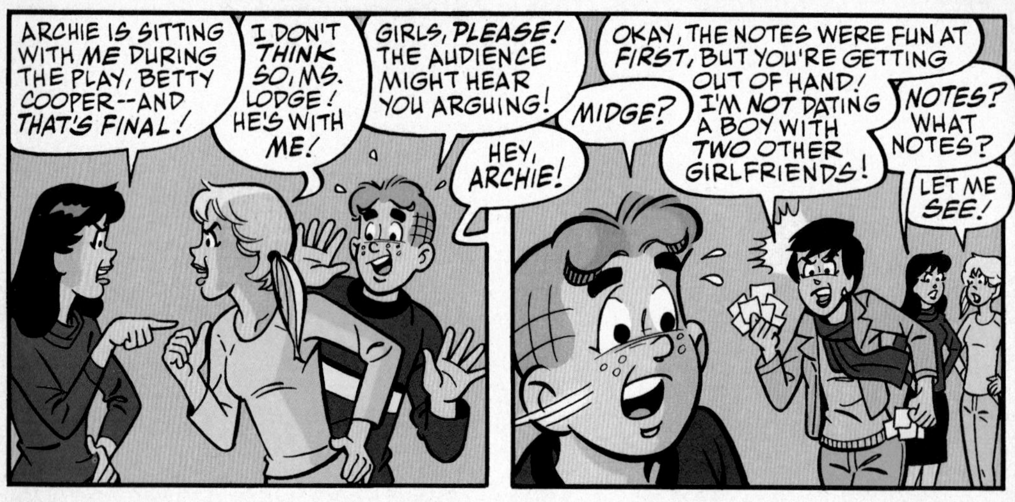
ARCHIE IS SITTING WITH ME DURING THE PLAY, BETTY COOPER--AND THAT'S FINAL!
I DON'T THINK SO, MS. LODGE! HE'S WITH ME!
GIRLS, PLEASE! THE AUDIENCE MIGHT HEAR YOU ARGUING!
HEY, ARCHIE!
MIDGE?
OKAY, THE NOTES WERE FUN AT FIRST, BUT YOU'RE GETTING OUT OF HAND! I'M NOT DATING A BOY WITH TWO OTHER GIRLFRIENDS!
NOTES? WHAT NOTES?
LET ME SEE!

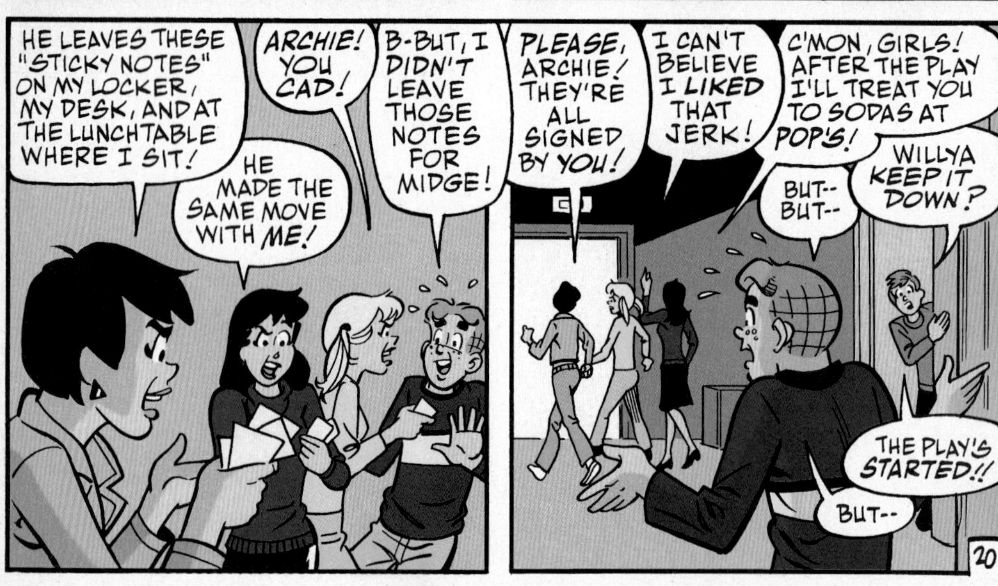
HE LEAVES THESE "STICKY NOTES" ON MY LOCKER, MY DESK, AND AT THE LUNCHTABLE WHERE I SIT!
HE MADE THE SAME MOVE WITH ME!
ARCHIE! YOU CAD!
B-BUT, I DIDN'T LEAVE THOSE NOTES FOR MIDGE!
PLEASE, ARCHIE! THEY'RE ALL SIGNED BY YOU!
I CAN'T BELIEVE I LIKED THAT JERK!
C'MON, GIRLS! AFTER THE PLAY I'LL TREAT YOU TO SODAS AT POP'S!
BUT-- BUT--
WILLYA KEEP IT DOWN?
THE PLAY'S STARTED!!
BUT--
20

AND OUT ON STAGE...

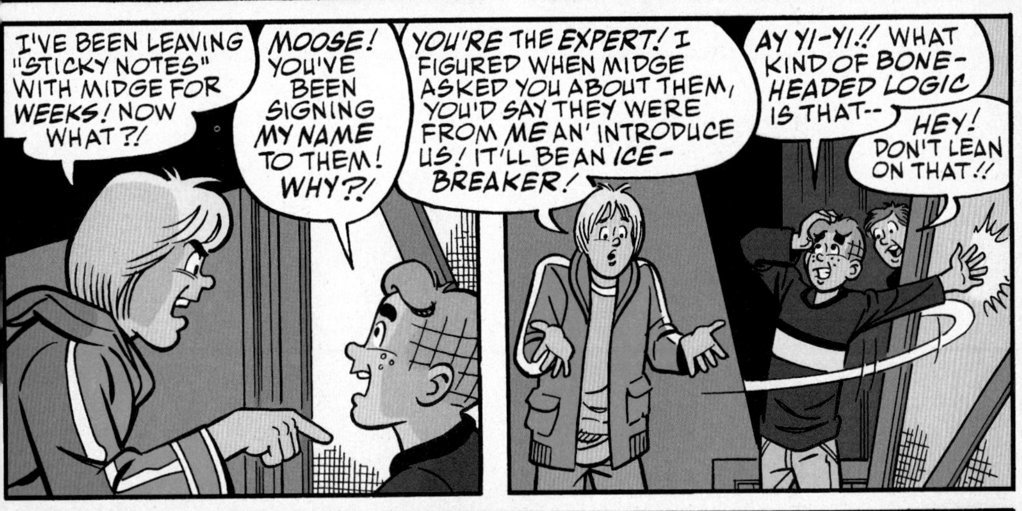

LATER...
WELL, MR. FIRST NIGHTER! HOW DID THE PLAY GO?

I DON'T THINK I'M GOING TO MAJOR IN THEATER, DAD!
I CAN'T TAKE THE DRAMA!

INTERESTING INTERPRETATION OF "CYRANO", DON'T YOU THINK?
I LIKED WHEN CYRANO AND ROXANNE CHASED THAT RED-HEADED KID THROUGH THE AUDIENCE!
SUPERINTENDENT HAVERHILL-! I HOPE YOU ENJOYED THE SHOW--

--DESPITE THE, ER... MINOR MISHAPS!
I DON'T KNOW ABOUT YOU, WEATHERBEE... YOU CAN'T SEEM TO CONTROL A STUDENT IN A PLAY... OR TO COOPERATE WITH A NEW TEACHER PROPOSING A NEW COURSE!
LET'S GO, DRIVER!

HOW'D HAVERHILL KNOW ABOUT BILL NEE'S PROPOSAL...?

!
22

GREAT BALLS OF FIRE! DOES HAVERHILL HAVE A SPY IN MY SCHOOL?!
END

ARE YOU READY, GERALDINE ?
I'LL BE RIGHT WITH YOU, MARTHA-- LET ME GET MY PAPERS!
TEACHERS LOUNGE

ARE THEY ALL IN THEIR SEATS ?
Oh, YES. BUT THERE ARE ALWAYS A FEW WHO WON'T SIT STILL!

Sigh! WHAT CAN A TEACHER DO ?
WE TRY TO REACH OUT TO EACH ONE. YOU CAN ONLY HOPE FOR THE BEST!
CHEM LAB
REPORT
REPORT

SOMETIMES THEY CAN BE SO DISRESPECTFUL! Oh, WELL... SEE YOU LATER, GERALDINE!
Tch! LISTEN TO THEM! NOISY BUNCH!

EXCUSE ME, EVERYONE-- MAY I HAVE YOUR ATTENTION ?
MY NAME IS GERALDINE GRUNDY--
1

FRESHMAN YEAR PART 4 OF 5

OH, HELLO, GLADYS! ARE YOU HERE ALONE FOR PARENT-TEACHER NIGHT, OR--?

FORSYTHE IS WORKING LATE... AT THE JOB YOU ARRANGED! WE WERE WORRIED ABOUT WORK WHEN WE MOVED BACK HERE.

THANK YOU FOR RECOMMENDING HIM FOR THAT JOB AT YOUR COOKWARE COMPANY. WE'RE HAPPY TO BE BACK IN RIVERDALE. THOUGH I'M CONCERNED ABOUT JUGHEAD...

WHAT'S THE PROBLEM?

I THOUGHT MOVING BACK TO RIVERDALE MIGHT MEAN AN IMPROVEMENT IN HIS SCHOOLWORK, BUT IT HASN'T! MY BOY MAY BE A BIT LAZY, BUT HE HAS POTENTIAL!

I UNDERSTAND WHAT YOU MEAN, GLADYS. I WANTED TO SEND MY VERONICA TO A PRIVATE INSTITUTION, BUT SHE BEGGED TO GO TO A PUBLIC SCHOOL! FRANKLY, I THINK HER GRADES HAVE SUFFERED.

OUR KIDS ARE FRIENDS... MAYBE THERE'S SOME COMMON FACTOR DISTRACTING THEM FROM STUDYING?

... HE ALSO HAS A HABIT OF DAYDREAMING IN CLASS! THAT IS, WHEN HE'S NOT TEXT MESSAGING ONE OF HIS BUDDIES...
I SEE...
Uh-Huh.

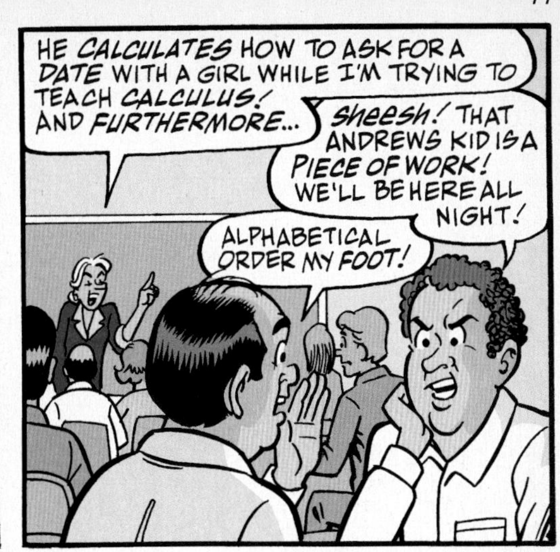
HE CALCULATES HOW TO ASK FOR A DATE WITH A GIRL WHILE I'M TRYING TO TEACH CALCULUS! AND FURTHERMORE...
Sheesh! THAT ANDREWS KID IS A PIECE OF WORK! WE'LL BE HERE ALL NIGHT!
ALPHABETICAL ORDER MY FOOT!

EXCUSE ME, MS. GRUNDY? WE REALIZE ARCHIE CAN BE A HANDFUL...
IN OTHER WORDS, WE GET THE IDEA...!

WE SHOULD MOVE ON TO ARCHIE'S OTHER INSTRUCTORS, OR WE COULD BE HERE ALL NIGHT!
FINALLY!
THANK YOU, MS. GRUNDY!

WELL, BUCKLE YOUR SEAT BELT, FRED... THAT WAS ONLY THE FIRST TEACHER...
WHAT NEXT?!

AT THAT VERY MOMENT...
I'VE GOT TO BE READY FOR ANY-THING!
4

WHO KNOWS WHAT MY TEACHERS WILL TELL MY PARENTS ?!
I'LL JUST FINISH MY HOMEWORK, AND MAKE SURE THAT THEY SEE ME STUDYING WHEN THEY GET HOME!
THE WEB
HISTORY
WEB

THIS WAY I CAN PREEMPT ANY...
BRRIIIINNGG
HISTORY

HI, ARCHIEKINS! IT'S VERONICA! YOU KNOW, I WAS THINKING...
...I'M SURE MY DAD IS GOING TO GIVE ME GRIEF AFTER TALKING TO MY TEACHERS...
MAYBE YOU SHOULD COME OVER AND WE'LL STUDY TOGETHER... WE COULD SHOW HIM WE'RE MAKING AN EFFORT!
BOTH MY FOLKS ARE AT SCHOOL, SO I'VE GOT TO STAY PUT, RONNIE. BESIDES--
The WEB
ELLE

--AFTER MY TEACHERS FINISH REVIEWING ME, I'M AFRAID MY FOLKS ARE GOING TO CRACK DOWN ON MY SOCIALIZING! SO IT'S BETTER IF I STUDY ALONE AND--
DING DONG

GOTTA GO, RON! SOMEONE'S AT THE DOOR!
SOMEONE'S AT THE DOOR? Hmmm...

THIS IS THE MAN YOU SHOULD BE TALKING TO!
WHASSUP?
PENCIL-NECK G?!
ARCHIE ANDREWS, ZANE ZAPPEN-- ZANE, ARCHIE! I'M SURE YOU'VE SEEN EACH OTHER AT SCHOOL...
DOUBLE A, I THOUGHT YOU'D BE ABLE TO TALK TO MY FRIEND ZANE, HERE.
Oh, SURE...
HI.
DUDE.
ME? ABOUT WHAT?
HE'S GOT A LITTLE PROBLEM! POOR GUY HAS TWO HOTTIES THAT ARE NUTS ABOUT HIM!
YEAH! CONNIE AND PENELOPE!
PENCILNECK-- I'D LOVE TO HELP, BUT I REALLY HAVE TO STUDY TONIGHT! AND THE LAST TIME I GAVE ADVICE, I REGRETTED IT!
DING DONG
DOOR.
BETTY?!
HI, ARCHIE! I KNOW YOU'RE NERVOUS ABOUT WHAT YOUR TEACHERS WILL TELL YOUR FOLKS, SO I THOUGHT I'D HELP YOU STUDY! OH-- I DIDN'T KNOW YOU HAD COMPANY!
HI, GUYS!
DUDE! SHE IS FIIIIINE!
WHAT'D I TELL YOU? DOUBLE A IS THE MAN!
6

MEAN-WHILE...
... AND THE ONLY SCIENCE ARCHIE SEEMS INTERESTED IN IS HIS CHEMISTRY WITH THE FEMALE STUDENTS!
Ah... THANK YOU, PROF. FLUTESNOOT. WE HAVE TO MOVE ON, DON'T WE, DEAR?
YES!

WHAT'S ARCHIE GOING TO MAJOR IN WHEN HE GETS TO COLLEGE ...? ANTICS? EVERY TEACHER HAS SOME MISADVENTURE TO REPORT!
NOW, FRED! MAYBE AN INCIDENT OR TWO IS BLOWN OUT OF PROPORTION! OH! THERE'S THE COOPERS!

WELL, HAL... THE GOOD NEWS IS THAT BETTY'S TEACHERS SAY SHE'S A FINE STUDENT -- BUT THE BAD NEWS IS THAT SHE'S FREQUENTLY DISTRACTED BY ARCHIE!
WE HAVE TO HAVE A SIT-DOWN WITH THAT GIRL! AND WE SHOULD SPEAK TO FRED AND MARY, AS WELL!

LET'S GET HOME, FRED, AND HAVE A HEART-TO-HEART WITH ARCHIE...
MARY -- THERE'S THE PRINCIPAL! LET'S GO -- BEFORE HE STARTS COMPLAINING ABOUT ARCHIE!
MR. WEATHER-BEE?

I RAN OUT OF NEXT FALL'S ACTIVITY FLYERS TO GIVE TO THE PARENTS. ARE THERE ANY MORE, OR SHOULD I PRINT OUT A FRESH BATCH?
UH... DO YOU THINK PRINTING MORE WOULD BE WASTE-FUL, JACKIE?

NOT IF WE'RE GOING TO USE THEM!
WELL, IN THAT CASE... GO AHEAD... PROCEED!
7

JUST LEAVE ME A MEMO IN MY E-MAIL THAT YOU THOUGHT PRINTING THE NEW FLYERS WAS A GOOD IDEA!
TCH! YOU'RE MAKING THE WORLD SAFE FOR BUREAUCRACY, MR. WEATHERBEE!
SAY, WALDO-- WHAT'S WITH YOU LATELY? I CAN TELL SOMETHING'S TROUBLING YOU--!
THERE IS! I FEEL LIKE I CAN TRUST YOU, GERALDINE. CAN I COUNT ON YOU TO BE DISCREET?

OF COURSE!
IT INVOLVES THE NEW TEACHERS THAT WERE TRANSFERRED HERE LAST SEMESTER. I HAVE GOOD REASON TO BELIEVE ONE OF THEM IS... BZZ... BZZ... BZZ...
A SPY?!
RIVERDALE HIGH SCHOOL

BETTY, I APPRECIATE YOU WANTING TO HELP ME...
BUT MY PARENTS THINK I'M STUDYING ALONE AND ARE GONNA BE PRETTY SORE TO SEE I HAVE FRIENDS OVER!
ANDREWS
SO WHY'D YOU INVITE THESE GUYS OVER?
AWESOME! "DOCTOR WHAT" IS ON!
NO HI-DEF? WASSUP WITH THAT?
I DIDN'T INVITE THEM! THEY--
DING DONG
GROAN! NOW WHAT?!
GET THE DOOR, ARCH -- I'LL GET OUT THE BOOKS AND PUT THE POP-CORN IN THE MICROWAVE!
JUGHEAD?! WHAT'RE YOU DOING HERE?!
EMERGENCY, PAL! WHILE MY FOLKS WERE OUT I WAS GOING TO ORDER A FEW PIZZAS--
--BUT THEY HAD ALL THE PIZZA PLACES PUT A BLOCK ON ANY DELIVERIES TO THE JONES RESIDENCE! IF THEY LIKE WHAT THEY HEAR AT SCHOOL, THE BAN WILL BE LIFTED! IF NOT, GULP NO MORE SNACKS!
SO YOU WANT TO USE MY ADDRESS TO ORDER A PIE!
IS SOMEONE ORDERING PIZZA?
HEY, GUYS! I DIDN'T KNOW YOU'D BE HERE. WHAT DO YOU WANT ON YOUR PIZZA?
SIGH! LEMME SEE IF BETTY WANTS ANY-THING...
9

I APPRECIATE YOUR CONCERN, GERALDINE... BUT PLEASE KEEP YOUR VOICE DOWN!
DO YOU REALLY THINK YOU'RE BEING SPIED ON? WHY?
BOILER ROOM
ALL I KNOW IS THAT PRIVATE CONVERSATIONS I HAVE -- ESPECIALLY THE DISAGREE-MENTS -- SEEM TO GET BACK TO SUPERINTENDENT HAVERHILL!
I TOLD YOU HE'S BEEN TOUGH ON ALL THE PRINCIPALS WHO'VE BEEN HERE!
HE SEEMS TO REALLY HAVE IT OUT FOR ME! EVER SINCE THE BIG NIGHT OF THE SCHOOL PLAY, I'VE NOTICED HE HAS INTIMATE KNOWLEDGE OF MY MEET-INGS!
I'VE NARROWED MY LIST OF SUSPECTS TO THE THREE TEACHERS WHO TRANSFERRED HERE AFTER THE HOLIDAY BREAK! BILL NEE HAS BEEN UNHAPPY WITH ME BECAUSE I WON'T APPROVE HIS NEW ELECTIVE...
JACKIE FLORES TEACHES A COMPUTER LAB--AND WOULD KNOW HOW TO HACK INTO MY COMPUTER!
SAM BURROWS IS FROM CENTRAL HIGH, BUT I CAN'T FIND A SINGLE PERSON THAT KNEW HIM THERE!
SAM BURROWS YOU SAY? HE'S BEEN ASKING A LOT OF QUESTIONS LATELY! IF I'M HAPPY HERE--
AH-HA! HE'S AFTER INFO--!
WELL THAT'S JUST AWFUL! THAT--THAT CREEP!
THERE, THERE, GERALDINE! I DON'T BLAME YOU FOR BEING UPSET. NO ONE LIKES A SPY!
I THOUGHT SAM WAS INTERESTED IN ME! BUT IF YOU'RE RIGHT, HE WAS JUST USING ME FOR INTEL!
:SIGH!: LIFE'S NOT FAIR, GERALDINE! WE SHOULD GET BACK, NOW... AND REMEMBER-- KEEP THIS ON THE Q.T.!
10

MEAN-WHILE...
CONNIE AND PENELOPE ARE BEST FRIENDS, BUT HAVE THIS RIVALRY OVER ME! THEY SEEM TO KNOW MY EVERY MOVE!
WHICH ONE IS THE NICE ONE?
YOU WANT THIS, JUG? I CAN'T EAT IT ALL.
PAL, WE'RE GONNA GET ALONG JUST FINE!
AS SOON AS WE FINISH EATING, YOU GOTTA GO! I DON'T WANT MY PARENTS TO FIND YOU HERE--
DING DONG
PIZZA
PIZZA

WHAT'S THIS?! A MID-WEEK PARTY, AND YOU DIDN'T INVITE ME?!
V-VERONICA! THERE'S NO PARTY!
Oh, REALLY? I SEE SODA, PIZZA, RIFF-RAFF...
HEY!!
MUNCH MUNCH
PIZZA
PIZZA

RONNIE! I WAS JUST STUDYING! HONEST!!
SORRY TO CRASH YOUR LITTLE PARTY, BETTY! I'LL SHOW MYSELF OUT, MR. ARCHIE ANDREWS!
DING DONG
STUDYING, Huh? AND I SUPPOSE THESE ARE YOUR TUTORS?!
?!!
I'M OUTTA HERE!!
11

WHO ARE YOU TWO ?!!
THAT'S CONNIE--
--AND THAT'S PENELOPE! IS ZANE HERE?

RONNIE!
THERE'S ZANE!
I TOLD YOU HE'D BE HERE!
IS THERE NO ESCAPE ??

RONNIE, PLEASE DON'T GO! IT'S ALL A MIS-UNDERSTANDING! LET ME EXPLAIN--
I'VE HEARD THAT BEFORE! GO BACK TO YOUR PALS 'N' GALS, ARCHIE!

GOOD LUCK WITH YOUR MIDTERMS, ARCHIE!
BETTY--!
THEN AGAIN... MAYBE I WILL GO BACK IN AFTER ALL...

FRED, I'M CONCERNED ABOUT ARCHIE!

IF WE'RE TO BELIEVE HIS TEACHERS, OUR BOY IS IRRESPONSIBLE AT BEST-- A TROUBLEMAKER AT WORST!
WE'LL SEE IF HE'S RESPONSIBLE ENOUGH TO BE LEFT HOME ALONE TO STUDY...
12

VROOM VROOM-ROOM

SPUTTER! MARY, IF WE DON'T KEEP TABS ON OUR SON, WE MIGHT LOSE HIM TO THE STREETS LIKE THOSE HOODLUMS!
LET'S JUST GET HOME FRED...
RRR-RRRRRRR
WHAT IS IT, FRED?
DANG IT! IT WON'T START!
AT THAT MOMENT
REGGIE! WHAT'RE YOU DOING HERE?
WORD GETS AROUND! MY REGGIE-SENSE CAN ALWAYS FIND A PARTY I'M NOT INVITED TO!
I SAW HIM FIRST!
NO! I DID!
MAN! I GOTTA GET AWAY FROM THEM!
YEAH, I SHOULD'VE LEFT-- BUT SOMEONE HAS TO KEEP AN EYE ON RONNIE!
SHEESH! HOW DID THIS HAPPEN?! MY FOLKS WILL FREAK WHEN THEY SEE THEIR HOME TURNED INTO A RAVE!
HOW DO I GET RID OF EVERY-ONE!?
ALLYSA! HOW'D YOU WIND UP HERE?
LIKE EVERYONE ELSE I READ ABOUT IT ON "GREG'S LIST" ONLINE! NO ONE ESCAPES THEIR NOTICE!
MY FRIEND ETHEL GOES TO SCHOOL WITH THE KID WHO LIVES HERE!
13

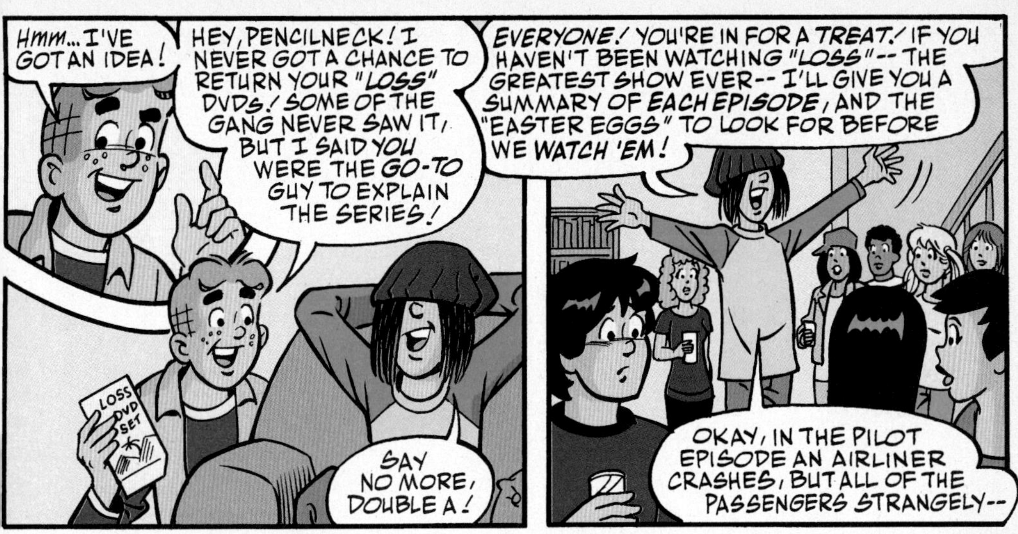
HMM... I'VE GOT AN IDEA!
HEY, PENCILNECK! I NEVER GOT A CHANCE TO RETURN YOUR "LOSS" DVDS! SOME OF THE GANG NEVER SAW IT, BUT I SAID YOU WERE THE GO-TO GUY TO EXPLAIN THE SERIES!
LOSS DVD SET
SAY NO MORE, DOUBLE A!
EVERYONE! YOU'RE IN FOR A TREAT! IF YOU HAVEN'T BEEN WATCHING "LOSS" -- THE GREATEST SHOW EVER -- I'LL GIVE YOU A SUMMARY OF EACH EPISODE, AND THE "EASTER EGGS" TO LOOK FOR BEFORE WE WATCH 'EM!
OKAY, IN THE PILOT EPISODE AN AIRLINER CRASHES, BUT ALL OF THE PASSENGERS STRANGELY--

--DISAPPEAR?

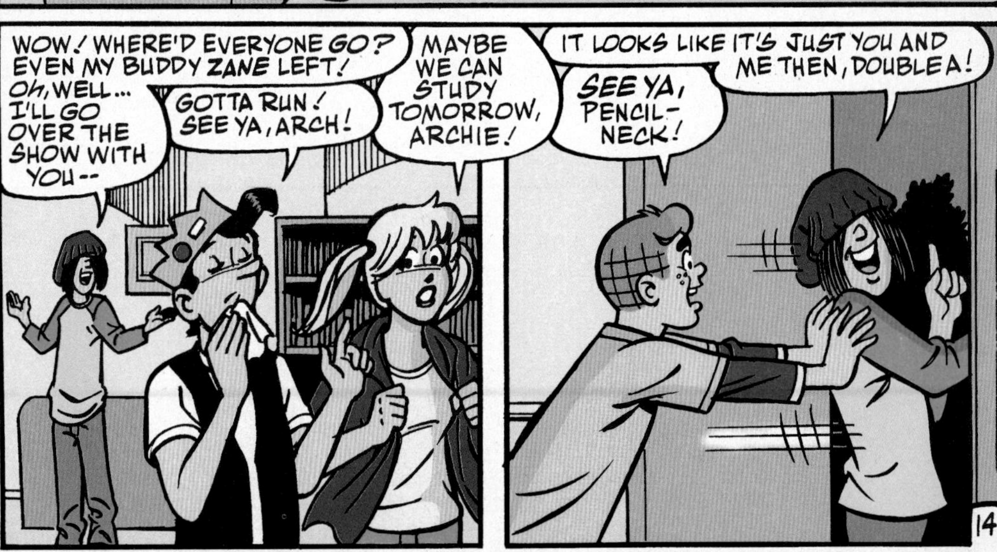
WOW! WHERE'D EVERYONE GO? EVEN MY BUDDY ZANE LEFT! OH, WELL... I'LL GO OVER THE SHOW WITH YOU --
GOTTA RUN! SEE YA, ARCH!
MAYBE WE CAN STUDY TOMORROW, ARCHIE!
IT LOOKS LIKE IT'S JUST YOU AND ME THEN, DOUBLE A!
SEE YA, PENCIL-NECK!
14

WHEW! I'M EXHAUSTED! BUT I'VE GOTTA CLEAN UP AND GET IN A LITTLE STUDYING BEFORE MY FOLKS GET BACK!
SHORTLY...
GASP ARCHIE FELL ASLEEP STUDYING!
AND HE EVEN TIDIED UP THE HOUSE, TOO! MAYBE WE WERE TOO HASTY WORRYING ABOUT HIM!
ZZZ! EH--MOM! DAD! WHERE HAVE YOU--

WE RAN OUT OF GAS--AND MY CELL HAD NO SIGNAL! WE HAD TO WALK TO THE GAS STATION!
MEANWHILE, YOUR TEACHERS HAD CHOICE THINGS TO SAY ABOUT YOU, YOUNG MAN...
TH-THEY DID?
...BUT I'LL GIVE YOU THE BENEFIT OF THE DOUBT. WE THINK YOU'RE A GOOD BOY WHO FINDS HIMSELF IN SITUATIONS BEYOND HIS CONTROL--!
YOU THINK ?!
WE KNOW, DEAR. THERE ARE SOME BAD KIDS OUT THERE, BUT YOU, YOU'RE NOT ONE OF THEM.
I'LL BE BACK DOWN IN A MINUTE!

EEEK!

SORRY... I MUST'VE DOZED OFF WHEN I CAME UP HERE TO HIDE OUT! DUDE--ARE CONNIE AND PENELOPE GONE YET?

AND SO, ALTHOUGH SPRING IS DEFINITELY IN THE AIR, THE FOLLOWING DAYS ARE BUSY ONES AT RIVERDALE HIGH -- THIS DAY IN PARTICULAR...
THE PROPER VERB TENSES WOULD BE WRITTEN LIKE THIS...
PSST! HEY, KID! I DIDN'T KNOW YOU COULD DRAW--!
YEAH! I WANNA BE A CARTOONIST!
COOL! IS THAT THE TEACHER? HA!
ANDREWS! CLAYTON! GET UP HERE AND BRING THAT DRAWING WITH YOU!
I'LL SEE YOU AFTER ART CLASS, MIDGE!
LATER, NANCY!
D-UH! I OVERHEARD THAT YOU'RE GOING TO ART CLASS! I'M THE... UH... MODEL TODAY. D-UH, THAT'S IT! THE MODEL!
REALLY? THEN YOU CAN WALK ME THERE! MY NAME IS MIDGE!
I'M... UH... MOOSE. CARRY YOUR BOOKS?
16

THAT'S A LOVELY TUNE!
UH-- THANKS!
WEREN'T YOU AT ARCHIE ANDREWS' HOUSE THE OTHER NIGHT?
IF I RECALL CORRECTLY, I WAS PREOCCUPIED WITH A PIZZA DELIVERY SITUATION THAT NIGHT!
RIVERDALE HIGH SCHOOL est. 1941
WORKED OUT IN MY FAVOR, I'M HAPPY TO SAY!
HEY, RONNIE! I DON'T WANT TO BE RIVALS!
ME NEITHER, BETS -- I'M SORRY WE ARGUED AT ARCHIE'S HOUSE THE OTHER NIGHT!
I'D RATHER BE FRIENDS THAN FIGHT OVER A GUY!
RIGHT ON!
ALL RIGHT, STUDENTS! WE HAVE A GUEST SPEAKER FOR SCIENCE CLASS TODAY...
DR. MASTERS OF THE HASKELL MEDICAL CENTER WILL SPEAK ABOUT CAREERS IN THE HEALTH SCIENCES...
HI, EVERY-ONE!
I HOPE TO ENLIGHTEN YOU ALL ABOUT THE MEDICAL PROFESSION...

CAN I GET A VOLUNTEER TO HELP ME PASS OUT SOME LITERATURE?
HERE, DR. MASTERS!
NO! OVER HERE, DR. MASTERS!!
I'M HELPING DR. MASTERS, COOPER!
MY APOLOGIES, DR. MASTERS! BUT WHAT DO YOU PRESCRIBE TO A COUPLE OF LOVESICK TEENAGERS?
YOU ALWAYS HAVE TO GET YOUR WAY, RON!
WOW! YOU'RE GOING TO EAT ALL THAT? ARE YOU SURE YOU'RE GETTING ALL YOUR TOTAL NUTRITIONAL VALUE FOR THE DAY? I CAN LOOK IT UP FOR YOU ON MY LAPTOP.
DO TELL.
I WILL! LET ME SEE--HERO SANDWICH, FRUIT, CHIPS, SOFT DRINKS--ARE YOU HAVING DESSERT, OR IS THAT A SILLY QUESTION...?
JUGHEAD?!
WHERE'D THAT BOY GO?!

FINALLY! A LITTLE QUIET! I CAN EAT MY LUNCH IN PEACE!
YOUNG MAN! ARE YOU SUPPOSED TO BE OUT HERE? LET ME SEE YOUR SCHEDULE!
UH-OH!
SORRY I'M LATE, CLASS! I HAD TO GET SOME ART SUPPLIES FROM THE STORE-ROOM, AND...
ART
OOM
GOOD HEAVENS! WHAT'S THE MEANING OF THIS?!
BUT, MS. KANDINSKY! THIS IS OUR MODEL... RIGHT?!
UH, YEAH... MODEL!

DETENTION
QUIET

RULES
CHRRPPP!

OH, HELLO... WELL, YOU CAN SAY I'M BUSY... I'M MONITORING DETENTION. CAN I CALL YOU BACK?
ALL RIGHT, HOLD ON.
OKAY, EVERYONE... I'LL BE RIGHT BACK. HONOR SYSTEM, NOW, HEAR?
OKAY, CHUCK! HE'S GONE!
GOOD! I CAN GET BACK TO WORK ON MY MINI-COMIC!
OKAY, I'LL BITE-- WHAT ARE MINI-COMICS?
THEY'RE MY HOMEMADE COMICS I MAKE WITH A COPIER! I REDUCE THE ART, FOLD THE PAPER, MAKE AS MANY COPIES AS I WANT, STAPLE THEM AND BAM!-- INSTANT COMIC BOOK!
CHUCK IS GOING TO DO A COMIC ABOUT US!
I'M THINKING OF CALLING IT "DETENTION COMICS".
IT'LL BE TRUE TALES OF GIRLS FIGHTING OVER A DOCTOR--
--A GOURMAND BUSTED FOR CUTTING LUNCH PERIOD--
WHAT'S A "GOURMAND"?
YOUR PICTURE IS NEXT TO THE DEFINITION IN THE DICTIONARY!
--AND A JOCK MOONLIGHTING AS AN ARTIST'S MODEL!
HEY! LIKE ME!
Detention COMICS
10
Detention COMICS

AND WILL THERE BE A STORY ABOUT TWO GEEKS CAUGHT GIGGLING OVER CARTOONS DURING CLASS?
Huh?!

REGGIE! WHAT'RE YOU DOING HERE?
I WAS HANGIN' WITH THE SENIORS IN THE CAFE-TERIA, AND WAS ABOUT TO HEAD UP TO POP'S...
ANYONE WANT TO JOIN ME...?

Oh! I'M SORRY! YOU CAN'T. YOU HAVE DETENTION!
JUST AS WELL-- THE SENIORS MAY NOT WANT A BUNCH OF FROSHES HANGIN' AROUND!
SEE YA, TROOPS!
IT WOULD'VE BEEN SO COOL IF MR. NEE CAUGHT REGGIE TAUNTING US AND GAVE HIM DETENTION!
HEY! WHAT HAPPENED TO MR. NEE? HE'S BEEN GONE AN AWFULLY LONG TIME!
I CAN'T REALLY TALK NOW. I DIDN'T EXPECT TO BE ASSIGNED TO DETENTION DUTY. I'LL BE OVER AS SOON AS I'M DONE HERE...
I GOTTA GO! SEE YOU LATER!
Ahem! BILL? I THOUGHT YOU WERE MONITOR-ING DETENTION?
DID YOU LEAVE THE STUDENTS UN-SUPERVISED?
SORRY, SIR--I HAD TO TAKE THIS CALL. "MY BAD" AS THE KIDS WOULD SAY!
I'LL GET BACK INSIDE ASAP!
21

YOU THINK I'M A SPY?! I'VE NEVER BEEN SO INSULTED!
TAKE IT EASY, BILL--
MR. NEE! PRINCIPAL WEATHERBEE!!

YUMPIN' YIMINY!!
ARE YOU ALL RIGHT, SON?
VRROOAARR

THEY WENT 'ROUND 'N' 'ROUND ME!
TAKE IT EASY, REGGIE... THE WORST IS OVER! WE'VE ALERTED THE POLICE!

I WANNA GO HOME!
COME INSIDE AND WE'LL CALL YOUR PARENTS TO PICK YOU UP!

I SAW THE ONE I ASSUMED WAS THE LEADER ASK YOU SOMETHING -- WHAT DID HE SAY?
HE ASKED ME MY NAME...
...HE WANTED TO KNOW IF I WAS ARCHIE ANDREWS!
TO BE CONCLUDED.

FRESHMAN YEAR

PART 5 OF 5

WRITER: *BATTON LASH* PENCILS: *BILL GALVAN*
INKS: *BOB SMITH* LETTERING: *JACK MORELLI*
COLORING: *GLENN WHITMORE*
MANAGING EDITOR: *MIKE PELLERITO*
EDITOR/EDITOR-IN-CHIEF: *VICTOR GORELICK*

MAN, DOUBLE A! YOU ARE LIKE MR. RIVERDALE HIGH!
Oh, I DON'T KNOW ABOUT THAT, PENCIL-NECK! I'M ONLY A FRESHMAN!
GO BULLDOGS

BUT DUDE! EVERYONE KNOWS YOU!
WELL, I HAVE TO ADMIT, IT IS NICE TO HEAR SOME-ONE GIVE ME A SHOUT OUT FROM ACROSS THE HALL!
PUSH

ANDREWS!
IN MY OFFICE-- NOW!
CATCH YOU LATER, DOUBLE A!

GULP! WHAT HAVE I DONE NOW? I BET HE HEARD ME REFER TO HIM AS "The BEE!"
YOU MEAN YOU HAVEN'T HEARD ABOUT BILL, JACKIE--?
I HEARD HE ASKED FOR A TRANSFER FROM RIVERDALE. TOO BAD, SINCE WE BOTH STARTED HERE WITH SAM BURROWS AFTER THE HOLIDAY BREAK! IS THERE MORE?
JUST BETWEEN US, JACKIE, BILL IS LEAVING BECAUSE WEATHERBEE ACCUSED HIM OF BEING AN INFORMANT FOR SUPERINTENDENT HAVERHILL!
AN IN-FORMANT?! YOU'VE GOT TO BE KIDDING, GERALDINE!
2

NOT ONLY DID BILL PUT IN FOR A TRANSFER, BUT HE'S FILING A COMPLAINT WITH THE SCHOOL BOARD, AND MIGHT EVEN SUE FOR SLANDER!
I GOT THE IMPRESSION WALDO WAS DISTRACTED OF LATE, BUT STILL--! WHAT MAKES HIM THINK HE'S BEING SPIED ON?
WHENEVER THERE'S A PROBLEM WITH THE SCHOOL, OR A DISAGREEMENT WITH THE FACULTY, HAVERHILL SEEMS TO HAVE ALL THE INSIDE INFORMATION!
AND TO BE FAIR TO WALDO, EVER SINCE THE HOMECOMING GAME LAST NOVEMBER, HAVERHILL HAS TAKEN A DISLIKE TO HIM!
NOW THAT YOU MENTION IT, I DO RECALL HIM GIVING WALDO GRIEF OVER THAT SILLY MISHAP AT THE SCHOOL PLAY!
G'DAY, LADIES!
WALDO'S NOT PERFECT, BUT HE TRIES HIS BEST AND LOVES HIS JOB!
WHAT MAKES WALDO THINK BILL NEE IS THE SPY?
COME, COME, GREGER! DON'T DAWDLE... VE HAFF WORK TO DO!
YOU'RE THE BOSS, SVENSON.
WALDO NOTICED THE LEAKS BEGAN AFTER THE SCHOOL GOT NEW TEACHERS AFTER THE WINTER BREAK. THAT WOULD BE BILL, SAM BURROWS,
AND--
AND ME! RIGHT, GERALDINE!?
RIGHT, JACKIE.
3

I'M LATE FOR MY CLASS!
YEESH!
GOOD NEWS, PEOPLE!

I SIGNED UP TO HELP THE SENIOR CLASS WITH THEIR FAREWELL DANCE! IT'S GOING TO BE A FESTIVE OCCASION TO SEND OFF THE GRADUATING CLASS IN STYLE...

...AND I'M RECRUITING VOLUNTEERS TO HELP ME REALIZE MY VISION!
UH... YOUR VISION? IT'S THE SENIORS' DANCE, RONNIE... AND YOU'RE JUST A FRESHMAN!

BETTY, DAHLING! WHAT I'M TRYING TO DO IS SET A PRECEDENT! SOMEDAY WE'LL BE GRADUATING, AND I WANT TO SET THE BAR HIGH FOR OUR FAREWELL DANCE!
OUR FAREWELL DANCE? I CAN'T IMAGINE LIFE OUT OF HIGH SCHOOL!
RONNIE, IF YOU NEED ANY ART-WORK, COUNT ME IN!

OH, DO YOU DRAW?
YEAH! I'D LIKE TO BE A PROFESSIONAL ARTIST SOMEDAY!
H-HI! MY NAME'S CHUCK CLAYTON!

AND I'M NANCY WOODS. WHAT KIND OF ART DO YOU DO? PORTRAITS? LANDSCAPE? WATERCOLORS? OIL?
I'M A CARTOONIST! I WANT TO DO--
4

--COMICS?
AW, DON'T LET IT GET YOU DOWN, CHUCK!
COMICS ARE AN INDIGENOUS AMERICAN ART-FORM. SHE'S JUST UNAWARE!
I KNOW, DILTON. BUT FOR THE "UNAWARE", I SHOULD'VE EASED INTO THE WHOLE THING! I'VE BEEN DYING TO MEET NANCY, BUT I GOT NERVOUS AND DIDN'T THINK STRAIGHT!
CHUCK, YOU HAVE TO APPROACH WOMEN AS YOU WOULD SCIENCE! THERE'S PLENTY OF MYSTERY BEFORE DISCOVERING IF YOUR CHEMISTRY DOES INDEED WORK...
HEY, CHUCK!
RONNIE SAYS SHE COULD USE SOME SIGNS FOR THE DANCE. I KNOW YOU DO CARTOONS, BUT--
IT'S ALL GOOD, BETTY! WHAT-EVER RONNIE NEEDS!
GREAT! WE'RE GOING TO MEET AT THE CHOCK LIT SHOP AFTER SCHOOL TO DISCUSS OUR DUTIES.
Oh! WHO'S YOUR FRIEND, CHUCK?
BETTY COOPER, MEET MY MAN DILTON DOILEY! HE WAS THE FIRST KID I MET BACK IN SEPTEMBER! THIS GUY IS RIVERDALE HIGH'S VERY OWN MAD SCIENTIST!
HIYA, DILTON! Y'KNOW, I DO THINK I'VE HEARD PROF. FLUTESNOOT MENTION YOU. HE SAID YOU'RE A GENIUS!
5

GOBBA DOBBA HEY?
EXCUSE ME?

HINGA BINGA GING!
I HAVE NO IDEA WHAT HE'S SAYING!
DON'T WORRY. NEITHER DOES HE!
I'LL MEET YOU AT POP TATE'S AFTER SCHOOL, RONNIE!

--I'VE, um... GOT TO GET TO CLASS NOW!
GO FOR IT, GIRL!

HI, JUGHEAD! I KNOW DANCES AREN'T YOUR THING, BUT WE'RE ALL GOING OVER TO POP'S LATER FOR...

KLIK
KLIK
KLIK
KLICK
KLICK
KLIK
KLIK

DO YOU THINK YOU CAN HELP ME WITH SOMETHING?
SURE!
6

MY BUDDY ARCHIE GOT CALLED INTO THE PRINCIPAL'S OFFICE. WHILE HE'S WAITING FOR THE "BEE" TO SEE HIM, HE TEXTED ME TO HELP FIGURE OUT WHY HE'S THERE!
I'VE BEEN TEXTING HIM SOME OF THE RECENT STUNTS THAT MIGHT HAVE GOTTEN HIM IN TROUBLE. YOU'RE IN SOME OF HIS CLASSES-- MAYBE YOU CAN THINK OF SOMETHING I MISSED!
GEE, ARCHIE IN TROUBLE?
WHERE DO I START?!
TELL ME ABOUT IT!

Hmm... I'M GLAD JUG REMINDED ME! AND THAT WAS THIS WEEK? AMAZING HOW THEY GOT THE CLASSROOM CLEANED UP SO QUICKLY!
LET'S SEE WHAT ELSE JUG CAME UP WITH--!

Whew! THAT'S QUITE A LIST... AND THERE'S MORE TO COME...
ANDREWS!
?? Oh, MAN, I'M IN FOR IT NOW!

COME INTO MY OFFICE. SORRY TO KEEP YOU WAITING, BUT THERE WERE SOME CALLS THAT NEEDED IMMEDIATE ATTENTION, AND--

YOU KNOW, I DIDN'T START CALLING YOU "THE BEE"! I GOT IT FROM THE SENIORS!

TCH! WHAT ARE YOU TALKING ABOUT? LISTEN TO ME-- WHERE'S YOUR CELL PHONE?
?

I WANT YOU TO TAKE THIS NUMBER. IF YOU SEE SIGNS OF SOMEONE GIVING YOU TROUBLE, I WANT YOU TO CALL...

A SECURITY TEAM I HIRED WILL RESPOND IMMEDIATELY! I WANT TO AVOID ANY MORE INCIDENTS WITH THAT MOTORCYCLE GANG!
BUT, MR. WEATHERBEE... IT'S BEEN WEEKS SINCE THAT HAPPENED...

"I'M NOT TAKING ANY CHANCES WITH THEM COMING BACK. THOSE HOODLUMS HARASSED YOUR FRIEND MANTLE WHILE LOOKING FOR YOU! THE AUTHORITIES ARE WORKING TO LOCATE THE GANG..."

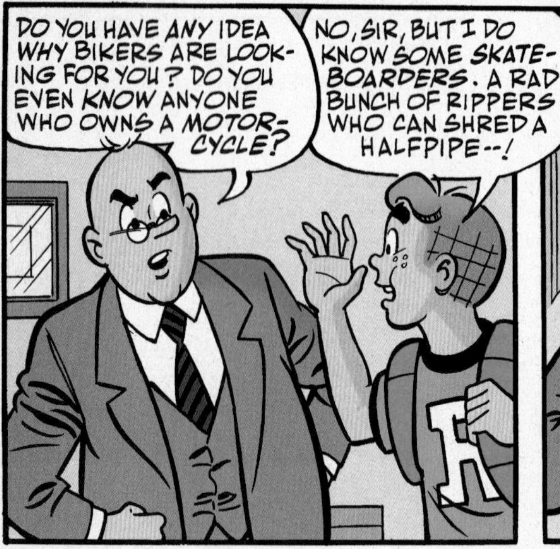
DO YOU HAVE ANY IDEA WHY BIKERS ARE LOOKING FOR YOU? DO YOU EVEN KNOW ANYONE WHO OWNS A MOTORCYCLE?
NO, SIR, BUT I DO KNOW SOME SKATEBOARDERS. A RAD BUNCH OF RIPPERS WHO CAN SHRED A HALFPIPE--!

Ahem! THAT WILL BE ALL, ANDREWS! YOU CAN GO NOW. AND REMEMBER, THAT NUMBER IS FOR EMERGENCIES ONLY!
UNDERSTOOD, SIR!
:GROAN: HE MUST THINK I'M STILL IN ELEMENTARY SCHOOL!

"RAD BUNCH OF RIPPED--??" WHO KNOWS WHAT THESE KIDS ARE TALKING ABOUT--
SAY! WHO'S CALLING ME "THE BEE"?!
EXCUSE ME, SIR!
YOU HAVE A CALL ON LINE ONE...
HOLD MY CALLS, MS. PHLIPS! WITH THE SCHOOL YEAR WINDING DOWN, I NEED TO OUTLINE SOME CURRICULUM IDEAS FOR THE FALL TERM, MEND SOME FENCES, ASSURE PARENTS, AND--

IT'S SUPERINTENDENT HAVERHILL, SIR!

Y-YES, SUPER-INTENDENT? HOW CAN I HELP YOU?
WEATHERBEE, I'M CALLING ABOUT YOUR TRIAL STATUS AS PRINCIPAL...
READ

AFTER CAREFUL CONSIDERATION FROM CLOSELY OBSERVING YOUR PERFORMANCE AT RIVERDALE HIGH THIS YEAR, AND TAKING INTO ACCOUNT SEVERAL INCIDENTS THAT OCCURRED UNDER YOUR WATCH, I'VE COME TO THIS CONCLUSION...
R

WE'RE HERE TO SEE THE PRINCIPAL, MS. PHLIPS.
WHAT'S THE PROBLEM, MS. NG?
10

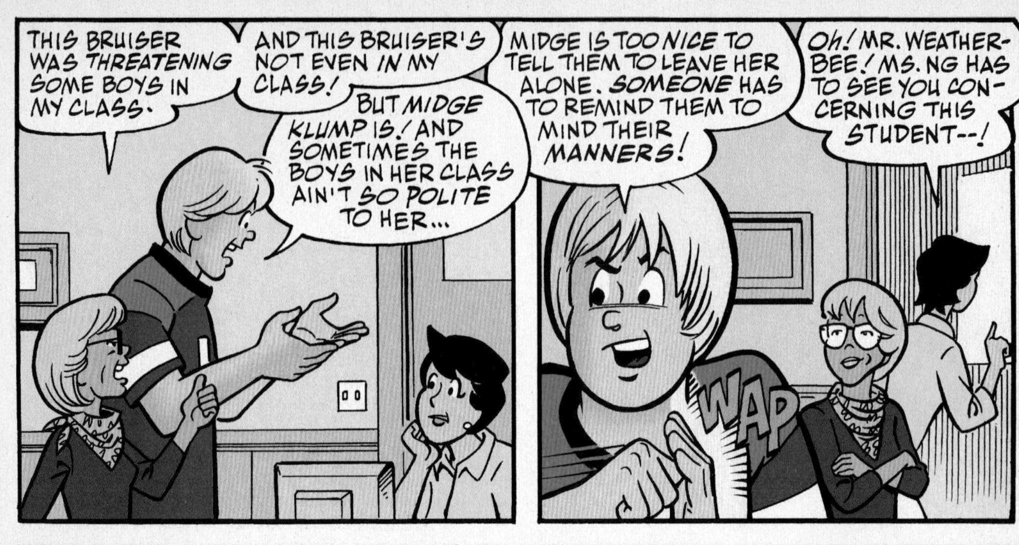
THIS BRUISER WAS THREATENING SOME BOYS IN MY CLASS.
AND THIS BRUISER'S NOT EVEN IN MY CLASS!
BUT MIDGE KLUMP IS! AND SOMETIMES THE BOYS IN HER CLASS AIN'T SO POLITE TO HER...
MIDGE IS TOO NICE TO TELL THEM TO LEAVE HER ALONE. SOMEONE HAS TO REMIND THEM TO MIND THEIR MANNERS!
WAP
Oh! MR. WEATHERBEE! MS. NG HAS TO SEE YOU CONCERNING THIS STUDENT--!

SIR?
I'LL BE OUT IN A MINUTE, MS. PHLIPS.
MR. WEATHERBEE? IS THERE SOMETHING WRONG?
HAVERHILL JUST INFORMED ME I'M BEING TERMINATED AS PRINCIPAL, EFFECTIVE AT THE END OF THIS TERM...

LATER, AFTER SCHOOL...
HEY, GANG! WAIT UP!
ARCHIEKINS! JUST THE PERSON I'M LOOKING FOR!
...SO I CAME UP WITH A LITTLE HOMING DEVICE THAT YOU CAN PUT ON A PET'S COLLAR SO IF IT GETS LOST, YOU HAVE A WAY TO TRACK IT. DO YOU HAVE A PET, BETTY?
Uh, BETTY? HELLO?
10

OKAY, OKAY! I ADMIT IT, CHUCK! I'VE NEVER READ A COMIC BOOK BEFORE!
NANCY, NANCY! HOW CAN YOU PASS JUDGMENT ON THEM, THEN?
I DON'T SEE THAT BIG GUY WHO'S USUALLY FOLLOWING YOU AROUND, MIDGE. DOES HE MAKE YOU NERVOUS?
OH, THAT'S MOOSE MASON, KIM. HE'S REALLY VERY SWEET--
--GALLANT, EVEN. IN A BARBARIC SORT OF WAY...
TELL ME, JUGHEAD-- WHAT DOES THAT "S" STAND FOR?
SECRET.
I'M SO HAPPY YOU'LL HELP ME WITH THE FARE-WELL DANCE, ARCHIE!
ANYTHING YOU WANT, RONNIE.
AND HERE I THOUGHT YOU'VE BEEN AVOIDING ME THESE LAST COUPLE OF WEEKS, BEING BUSY EVERY WEEKEND AND ALL...
TUT, TUT! MY SOCIAL CALENDAR IS JUST SUCH THAT I COULD BARELY FIT IN SCHOOL! BUT I CAN ALWAYS FIND TIME FOR MY ARCHIEKINS!
WOW!
I'M PLEASED TO SEE YOU SO ENTHUSIASTIC, ARCHIE! THE LODGE NAME HAS ALWAYS BEEN ASSOCIATED WITH EVENTS. I CAN ALWAYS USE A DEVOTED LACKEY-- I MEAN VOLUNTEER!
COOL!
I ENVISION A NEW STANDARD WHERE WE RAISE THE BAR HIGH FOR HIGH SCHOOL DANCES!
ARCHIE?
AWE-SOME!
11

THAT IS THE MOST BEAUTIFUL SIGHT I'VE EVER SEEN!
IS IT, ARCHIBALD? IS IT?
JUG! CHECK THIS OUT, BUD! IT'S EVERYTHING I'VE EVER DREAMT OF!!
TIME'S A'WASTIN'-- WE'VE GOT A MEETING AT THE CHOCKLIT SHOP-- AND WE'RE LATE!

YOU CAN HAVE MY HOMING DEVICE. EVEN THOUGH CARMEL IS JUST A KITTEN, YOU MIGHT WANT TO PUT IT ON HER COLLAR WHEN SHE STARTS GOING OUT!
THANK YOU, DILTON. BUT SHE'S GOING TO STAY AN INDOOR CAT!
BUT... I THINK I COULD PUT THIS TO GOOD USE IN OTHER WAYS!
HEY, RONNIE! I JUST WENT AHEAD TO SEE WHO'S AT THE CHOCKLIT SHOP--

--AND SAW THE PLACE IS PACKED! THERE'S NO PLACE TO SIT! HOW ARE WE GONNA HAVE A MEETING?!
NOT TO WORRY, SAMIR! I HAD REGGIE GO THERE TO HOLD A BOOTH FOR THE TWO OF US!
OH, YEAH... AND I RAN INTO REGGIE!
SORRY, RONNIE-- OUR UPPER CLASS-MATES LET ME KNOW IN NO UNCERTAIN TERMS THEY HAVE A "NO HOLDING" POLICY!
12

YARGH! IF YOU WANT SOMETHING DONE, YOU'VE GOTTA DO IT YOURSELF!
BUT RON--THOSE KIDS WOULDN'T BUDGE! AND THEY GOT REAL NASTY AND SAID--

SPARE ME THE SAD EXCUSES, REGINALD! EVERYONE?
GIVE ME FIVE MINUTES.
POP

EXACTLY FIVE MINUTES LATER...
COME ON IN, GANG! A COUPLE OF BOOTHS OPENED UP!
POP

RONNIE! HOW?!
I OFFERED TO TREAT OUR UPPER CLASSMATES TO BURGERS AND SODAS IN EXCHANGE FOR SOME SEATING PRIVILEGES...YOU'D BE SURPRISED HOW MANY SEATS WE COULD'VE HAD!

DON'T BE SURPRISED--THIS IS CALLED A BUSINESS EXPENSE! WE PARTY PLANNERS DO IT ALL THE TIME! NOW LET'S GET TO WORK!
MENU

MEANWHILE, ACROSS TOWN...
I'M GLAD YOU'RE HERE. I WANT YOU TO KNOW I CALLED WEATHERBEE TO GIVE HIM THE BOOT--
SUPERINTENDENT HAVERHILL

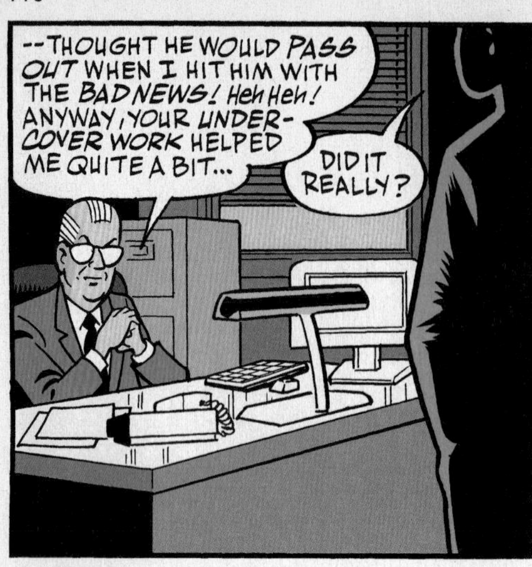
--THOUGHT HE WOULD PASS OUT WHEN I HIT HIM WITH THE BAD NEWS! Heh Heh! ANYWAY, YOUR UNDER-COVER WORK HELPED ME QUITE A BIT...
DID IT REALLY?

OF COURSE! I SUSPECTED THAT WEATHERBEE WAS A BUNGLER, AND NOT FIT TO RUN A HIGH SCHOOL, BUT I NEEDED SOMEONE THERE EVERY DAY TO GIVE ME A FIRST-HAND ACCOUNT!

WEATHERBEE JUST WASN'T UP TO THE JOB! AMONG HIS MANY ADMINI-STRATIVE SHORTCOMINGS, HE HAD A SCHOOL OUT OF CONTROL, WITH BULLIES ROAMING THE HALLS, A BIKE GANG TRES-PASSING ON SCHOOL PROPERTY, STUDENTS RUNNING WILD IN THE HALLS...
...NOT TO MENTION BEING UNCOOPERATIVE TO FACULTY MEMBERS AND INTOLERANT OF THEIR SUGGESTIONS!

GOOD RIDDANCE TO BAD RUBBISH, I SAY!
WITH ALL DUE RESPECT, SIR...

I THOUGHT I MADE IT CLEAR IN MY REPORTS THAT WHAT I SAW IN WEATHERBEE WAS A MAN WHO DEEPLY CARED FOR HIS STUDENTS AND STRIVED TO DO THE BEST FOR RIVERDALE HIGH!
14

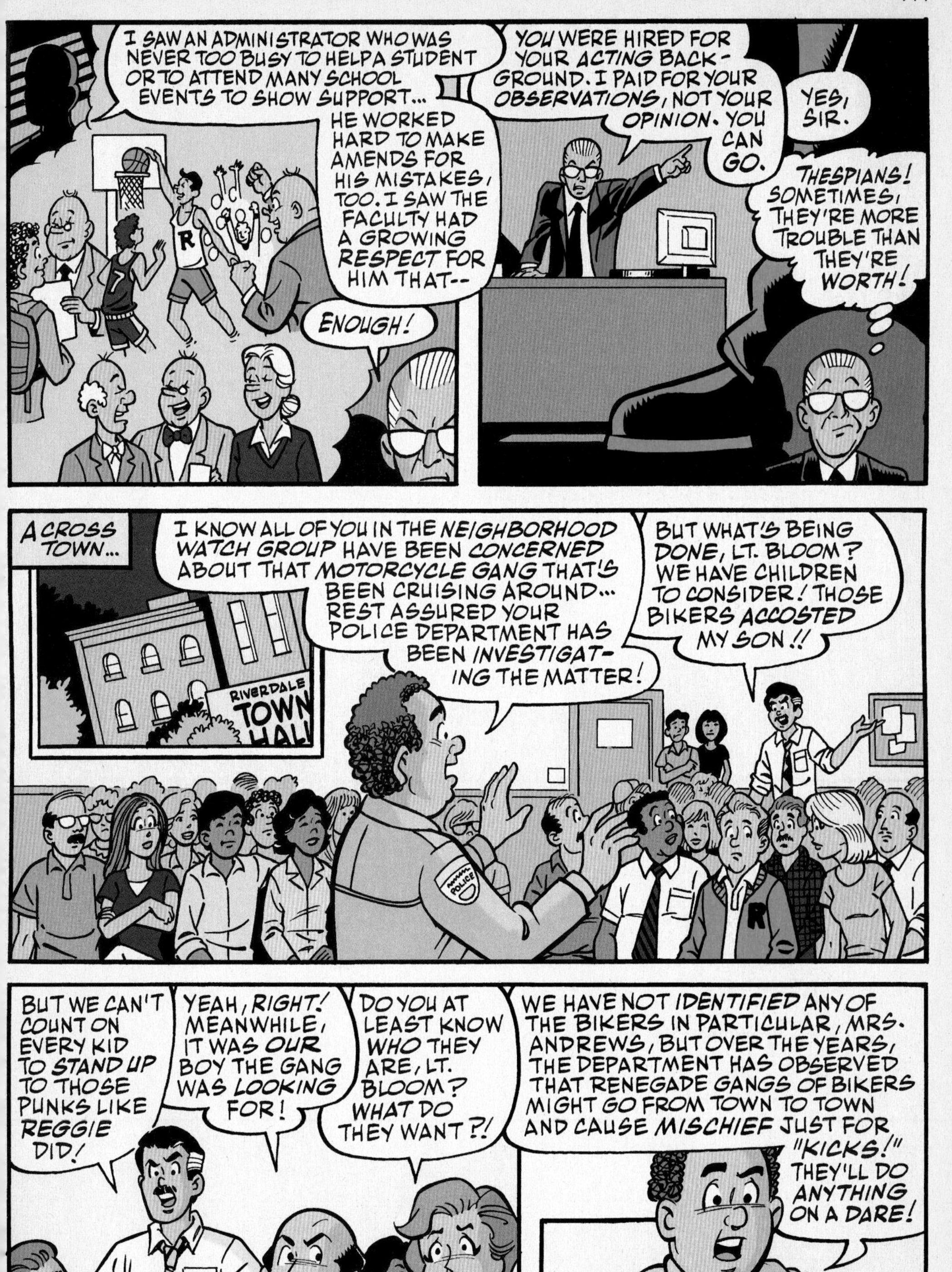
I SAW AN ADMINISTRATOR WHO WAS NEVER TOO BUSY TO HELP A STUDENT OR TO ATTEND MANY SCHOOL EVENTS TO SHOW SUPPORT...
HE WORKED HARD TO MAKE AMENDS FOR HIS MISTAKES, TOO. I SAW THE FACULTY HAD A GROWING RESPECT FOR HIM THAT--
ENOUGH!
YOU WERE HIRED FOR YOUR ACTING BACK-GROUND. I PAID FOR YOUR OBSERVATIONS, NOT YOUR OPINION. YOU CAN GO.
YES, SIR.
THESPIANS! SOMETIMES, THEY'RE MORE TROUBLE THAN THEY'RE WORTH!
ACROSS TOWN...
I KNOW ALL OF YOU IN THE NEIGHBORHOOD WATCH GROUP HAVE BEEN CONCERNED ABOUT THAT MOTORCYCLE GANG THAT'S BEEN CRUISING AROUND... REST ASSURED YOUR POLICE DEPARTMENT HAS BEEN INVESTIGAT-ING THE MATTER!
BUT WHAT'S BEING DONE, LT. BLOOM? WE HAVE CHILDREN TO CONSIDER! THOSE BIKERS ACCOSTED MY SON!!
RIVERDALE TOWN HALL
POLICE
BUT WE CAN'T COUNT ON EVERY KID TO STAND UP TO THOSE PUNKS LIKE REGGIE DID!
YEAH, RIGHT! MEANWHILE, IT WAS OUR BOY THE GANG WAS LOOKING FOR!
DO YOU AT LEAST KNOW WHO THEY ARE, LT. BLOOM? WHAT DO THEY WANT?!
WE HAVE NOT IDENTIFIED ANY OF THE BIKERS IN PARTICULAR, MRS. ANDREWS, BUT OVER THE YEARS, THE DEPARTMENT HAS OBSERVED THAT RENEGADE GANGS OF BIKERS MIGHT GO FROM TOWN TO TOWN AND CAUSE MISCHIEF JUST FOR "KICKS!" THEY'LL DO ANYTHING ON A DARE!
15

THE GANG HAS NOT BEEN SEEN SINCE THE INCIDENT AT THE SCHOOL. THE DEPARTMENT BELIEVES THEY'VE MOVED ON AND LEFT RIVERDALE...
POLICE
YOU RODE IN RIVERDALE? HOW CUTTING EDGE CAN YOU GET?
HAW-HAWW-HAW!!
HEY! THAT BURG DIDN'T KNOW HOW TO HANDLE US!
LUCY A'S ROAD HOUSE

WADDYA DO, REV YER ENGINES AN SCARE THE LI'L OLD LADIES!?
HAW-HAW-HAW!
IF YOU GUYS HAD ANY GUTS, YOU'D CRASH AN EVENT!
WE BROKE UP A FOOTBALL GAME AT PEMBROOKE HIGH--AND GOT OUT BEFORE THE COPS ARRIVED!
LEMME KNOW WHEN YOU BOYS GET SOME BACK-BONE!
THEN MAYBE YOU CAN RIDE WITH US!
LEE! YOU SHOULD HAVE TOLD THEM ABOUT US IN THAT SCHOOL-YARD IN RIVER-DALE--

AND WHAT? TELL THEM WE RAN CIRCLES AROUND SOME KID? AND IT WASN'T THE ONE MY BROTHER WAS LOOK-ING FOR!
HEY, LEE! MY BUDDY FOGARTY GOES TO THAT SCHOOL AND SAYS THERE'S A DANCE COMIN' UP!
OH, YEAH? Y'KNOW, FELLAS, WE GOT SOME UNFINISHED BUSINESS TO TAKE CARE OF IN RIVERDALE...
I OWE MY DOPEY BROTHER THAT MUCH, RIGHT?
RIGHT, LEE! HAHAHAHA!
16

AND ON THE DAY OF THE DANCE...
HEY, YOU KIDS! GO SOMEWHERE ELSE! YOU'RE NOT GONNA USE MY CURB AS A RAMP ALL SUMMER LONG!
MOM McCANN'S DINER
OPEN
FINE! WE'LL GO TO ANOTHER PLACE TO HANG OUT AND EAT--
PENCILNECK!! WATCH OUT!!
VROOM
HAHAHA HAHA!!
THAT WAS A CLOSE ONE!
BUT OH, NO-- THE BIKERS ARE BACK IN TOWN!!
WHAT DO THEY WANT?!
GROAN HOW DID I LET RONNIE TALK ME INTO THIS? SHE PUT ME TO WORK AND THEN IGNORES ME! WHY AM I HERE?
WHERE'S THE FOOD?
I FEEL SO USED! AND RONNIE BARELY EVEN RESPONDED TO THE GIFT I GAVE HER! AND IF SHE THINKS FLIRTING WITH A SENIOR IS GOING TO MAKE ME JEALOUS, WELL, SHE'S NUTS!!
BY THE WAY, JUG-- HAVE YOU SEEN HER?
I'LL GO LOOK-- RIGHT NOW!
17

HEY, DILTON, CAN YOU MIND THE TICKET TABLE WHILE I LEAVE FOR A FEW MINUTES?
OF COURSE, BETTY. NO PROBLEM--
--TAKE YOUR TIME.
DO YOU WANT TO DANCE, ARCHIE? THIS IS SUCH A NICE SONG!
WELLLL, I'M SUPPOSED TO BE TROUBLE-SHOOTING...
AH, LET'S GO, BETTS!
I GUESS THIS IS WALDO'S "FAREWELL DANCE". FRANKLY, I'M SURPRISED HE'S EVEN HERE!
I'M NOT! THE SCHOOL AND THE KIDS MEAN A LOT TO HIM!
DANCE
BUT ONE THING PUZZLES ME... WHO ARE THOSE MEN WALDO IS TALKING TO?
IF I DIDN'T KNOW BETTER, JUG-HEAD P. JONES, I'D SAY YOU WERE AVOIDING ME!
ALL I WANT TO KNOW IS WHAT THE "S" ON YOUR SHIRT MEANS!
SNACK?
BETTY, YOU LOOK DIFFERENT TONIGHT!
OH, I CHANGED MY HAIRSTYLE! I THOUGHT I'D TRY IT FOR A WHILE...
...WHO KNOWS IF I'LL KEEP IT...
FOR WHAT IT'S WORTH, BETTY, IT'S YOU--
OH, MY GOODNESS!

VROOM VROOM
FAREWELL DA
TROUBLE
LEE! THAT'S HIM! THERE'S ANDREWS!
GRAB HIM AND LET'S GET OUTTA HERE!
THE OTHERS CAN MEET US LATER!
JUST THEN, THE AUDITORIUM DOORS SLAM SHUT!
BAM BAM SLAM
--PREVENTING THE OTHER BIKERS FROM LEAVING!
WHO ARE THESE GUYS?
@#$%! WE'RE TRAPPED!
SECURITY
SECURITY

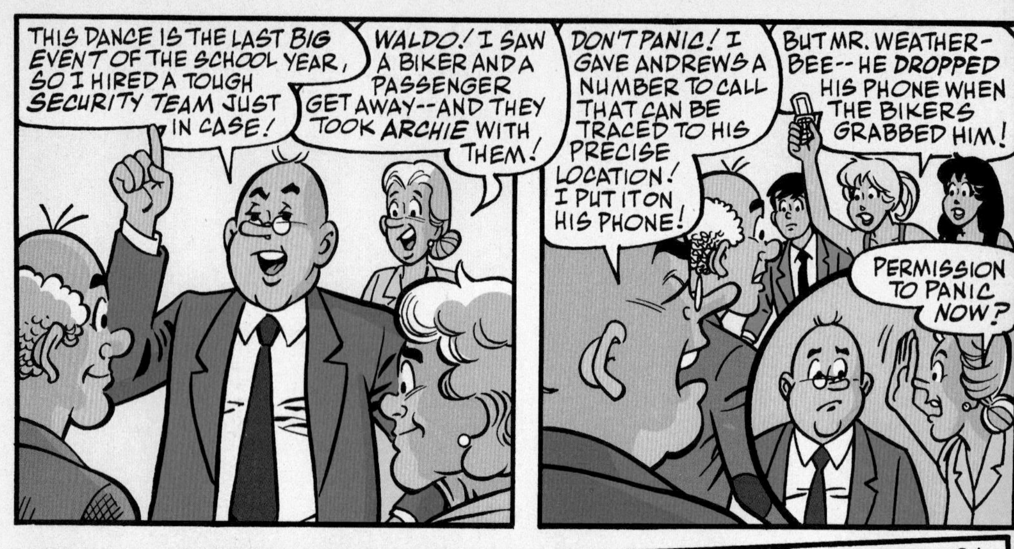
THIS DANCE IS THE LAST BIG EVENT OF THE SCHOOL YEAR, SO I HIRED A TOUGH SECURITY TEAM JUST IN CASE!
WALDO! I SAW A BIKER AND A PASSENGER GET AWAY--AND THEY TOOK ARCHIE WITH THEM!
DON'T PANIC! I GAVE ANDREWS A NUMBER TO CALL THAT CAN BE TRACED TO HIS PRECISE LOCATION! I PUT IT ON HIS PHONE!
BUT MR. WEATHERBEE-- HE DROPPED HIS PHONE WHEN THE BIKERS GRABBED HIM!
PERMISSION TO PANIC NOW?

DOWNTOWN...
WHAT'S YOUR PROBLEM, MAN? WHAT DO YOU WANT WITH ME?
A LITTLE PAYBACK, FROSH!
JARED McGERK!
YOU CAUSED ME A LOT OF TROUBLE, PUNK! I'M GONNA--
WAITA-MINNIT!

YOU'VE GOT TO BE KIDDING ME! THIS IS THE GUY YOU'VE BEEN HARPING ABOUT ALL YEAR!? THE WAY YOU DESCRIBED HIM, I WAS EXPECTING A SIX-FOOT TALL FOOTBALL LINEBACKER!
AWW, BUT LEE-- YOU DON'T UNDERSTAND! HE--
HAWHAWHAWHAW! LITTLE BROTHER-- YOU'RE SUCH A LOSER! YOU LET THIS TWERP GET THE BEST OF YOU?? WAH HAHA HAHA!
TWERP?
FORGET HER, FROSH! I'M GONNA GIVE YOU SOMETHING YOU'LL ALWAYS REMEMBER!
20

STAY AWAY FROM THAT BOY AND PUT YOUR HANDS IN THE AIR!!
WOW, OFFICER! HOW'D YOU MANAGE TO FIND ME?!
WE GOT A TIP FROM A CONCERNED CITIZEN!
PENCIL-NECK G!!
DOUBLE A! THAT BIKER ALMOST RAN ME DOWN! WHEN I SAW HER AGAIN WITH YOU, ME AND MY BROS CALLED 911-- I WASN'T GONNA LET HER GET AWAY WITH BEING SO UNCOOL!

AND WITHIN A WEEK...
MR. HAVERHILL... WE WERE CONTACTED BY AN INDIVIDUAL YOU HIRED TO KEEP AN EYE ON PRINCIPAL WEATHERBEE DURING SCHOOL HOURS.
RIVERDALE SCHOOL DISTRICT OFFICES

WE FOUND THIS REPORT QUITE INTERESTING, SINCE IT CONTRADICTS YOUR FINDINGS, AND YOUR EX-EMPLOYEE WAS MOVED ENOUGH TO CONTACT US BECAUSE HE FELT MR. WEATHERBEE WAS NOT GETTING A "FAIR SHAKE."
AFTER READING HIS REPORT AND WITNESSING MR. WEATHERBEE'S BEHAVIOR UNDER FIRE, WE AGREE. THE BOARD OVERRULES YOUR DECISION.
NOT ONLY DOES MR. WEATHERBEE STAY AS PRINCIPAL, BUT WE'VE ALSO VOTED UNANIMOUSLY TO NOT RENEW YOUR CONTRACT AS SUPERINTENDENT, MR. HAVERHILL!
THESPIANS! MORE TROUBLE THAN THEY'RE WORTH!

WELL, HERE IT IS, WALDO! THE LAST DAY OF SCHOOL! YOU SURVIVED YOUR FIRST YEAR!
I'M JUST VERY PLEASED THAT I'LL BE HERE FOR A SECOND ONE!
RIVERDALE HIGH SCHOOL est. 1941

I JUST WISH I'D LEARNED WHO WAS THE ONE SPYING ON ME. I REGRET OFFENDING BILL NEE, JACKIE FLORES, AND SAM BURROWS BY SUSPECTING THEM, BUT THE "LEAKS" STARTED ONCE THEY TRANSFERRED HERE IN FEBRUARY!
SPEAKING OF LEAKS...
WET FLOOR
21

SORRY, VEATHERBEE! THAT GREGER UPPED AN' QUIT LAST VEEK-- JOST LIKE THAT! I BAN DOIN' THE VORK OF TWO!
DON'T VORRY-- I MEAN DON'T WORRY, SVENSON! WE'LL GET YOU A NEW ASSISTANT!
NOW, WHOEVER THE SPY WAS, THEY HAD TO HAVE ACCESS TO MY PRIVATE CONVERSATIONS AND PHONE CALLS. I WOULDN'T BE SURPRISED IF THIS PERSON WENT THROUGH MY TRASH EVERY DAY! IT'S THE ONLY WAY SOME OF THE INFORMATION COULD POSSIBLY HAVE--
GREGER!
YOU MEAN THE JANITOR WAS THE SPY?
WHO BETTER TO FIND DIRT ON ME?
NO RUNNING IN THE HALLWAYS, YOUNG MAN!
HERE'S YOUR ORDER TO GO, SIR...
SAY! DON'T I KNOW YOU?
POP'S CHOCKLIT SHOPPE
ARE YOU ON TV?
I'VE DONE SOME COMMERCIALS, BUT I'M MOSTLY A THEATER ACTOR. IN FACT, I'M LEAVING RIVERDALE TO DO SUMMER STOCK IN NEW YORK...
REGGIE! DO YOUR PURLEY GATES IMITATION!
OKAY!
"LOVE ME TENDER, LOVE ME FAT, LOVE ME IN THE AUTOMAT!"
HA HA HA

HEY, KIDS! KEEP IT DOWN TO A RESPECTFUL ROAR! UNTIL I LEARN YOUR NAMES, I'M GONNA HOLD YOU ALL ACCOUNTABLE!
GEE! YOU THINK MR. TATE IS MAD AT US?
MAYBE WE SHOULD KEEP IT DOWN A LITTLE!
GOOD IDEA-- I DON'T WANT TO GET THROWN OUT! I LIKE IT HERE!
I NEVER GET A STRAIGHT ANSWER OUT OF YOU, MR. JONES!
SO I WON'T INQUIRE AS TO WHAT THAT "S" ON YOUR SHIRT STANDS FOR!
SWEET!
I ASKED PENCILNECK G TO JOIN US, BUT HE TOOK A RAIN-CHECK. BOY I OWE HIM!
I INVITED DILTON, BUT I THINK HE'S TOO SHY. WHEN HE HEARD THERE WOULD BE A CROWD, HE BACKED OFF!
ATTENTION, EVERYONE!
TODAY WAS THE LAST DAY OF SCHOOL. WE HAVE OFFICIALLY MADE IT THROUGH OUR FIRST YEAR OF HIGH SCHOOL! I PROPOSE A TOAST--
HERE'S MY TOAST!
ARCHIE ANDREWS! YOU ARE SOOO SOPHOMORIC!
SO? WITH OUR FRESH-MAN YEAR OVER...
...WE'RE OFFICIALLY SOPHOMORES!
HAHAHAHAHA!
:Sigh!: HOW LONG BEFORE SCHOOL STARTS AGAIN?
THE END UNTIL NEXT TERM!